How I Survived My Summer Vacation*

*And Lived to Write the Story

How I Survived My Summer Vacation*

* And Lived to Write the Story

Robin Friedman

Front Street / Cricket Books
Chicago

Library of Congress Cataloging-in-Publication Data
Friedman, Robin.
How I survived my summer vacation: and lived to write
the story/Robin Friedman.—1st ed.
p. cm.
Summary: Determined to write a novel during the summer before he
starts high school, thirteen-year-old Jackie struggles with his inability
to finish anything and with the advice of others.
ISBN 0-8126-2738-5
[1. Writing—Fiction. 2. Determination (Personality trait)—Fiction.]
I. Title.

PZ7. F89785 Ho 2000
[Fic]—dc21
99-058252

For my husband, Joel,
whose youthful stories provided
the spark for this book

How I Survived My Summer Vacation*

*And Lived to Write the Story

Chapter 1

"Out of all the things I could have done that morning, who would have guessed that waking up was the worst choice."

I stared at my words until they began to blur into strange black shapes. A great opening line for a novel, I thought foolishly, grinning like an idiot and feeling oh-so-pleased with myself.

My writing book said to get that all-important opening line down on paper. It had taken me a week just to think of it. That's O.K. The book said it wouldn't be easy. Well, I wish the book had said something about the second sentence, too. It spent a whole chapter on the opening line but didn't utter a peep about the second sentence.

The next five minutes passed in slow motion while I struggled to think of another line. I stared out my window for inspiration, but our overgrown backyard offered up nothing. I looked at the roof, the fence, the driveway, the old oak tree, the herb garden.

Nothing. Absolutely nothing.

My eyes came to rest on the writing book next to me on the desk. *GET RICH QUICK!* the title screamed in bold, gold-stamped letters. *Write a Bestseller in Less Than a Year* it promised underneath the title in smaller type.

Less than a year? At this rate it would take a century.

I looked around my room at the clothes on the floor, the old posters on the wall, the model airplane I built when I was eight. I stared at my goldfish, who swam quietly in the bubbling water.

"What do you think, guys?" I asked them.

They didn't answer.

I sighed.

If I was really going to write a novel this summer, then I had to write a second sentence. And a third, and a fourth, and a thousandth. But it was hopeless as usual, I thought in my patented grumpy way.

A few more minutes passed as I silently groped for inspiration. A bushy-tailed squirrel raced across the lawn under my window, momentarily giving me an idea, but as soon as it was gone, so was my idea.

"This isn't working," I said out loud. I pulled out the sheet of paper from my typewriter. I read the great opening line again, sighed again, and tore the paper into a million pieces. I fed another sheet of paper into the typewriter, trying to control my rapid breathing.

Stay calm, I told myself. It's going to be O.K. Panicking is for wimps.

The aroma of coffee began to drift into my room, which could only mean one thing. Dad was downstairs in the kitchen, preparing his signature breakfast dish: scrambled tofu with fig sauce.

Though all kids claim to have this problem, my parents are a *true* embarrassment to me.

"Jackie! Grub's ready! Come on down!"

It was Dad, ready for breakfast at 9 A.M. on the dot, as usual. He always cooks precisely on the hour, whether it's lunch at 12 noon or dinner at 6 P.M. Mom says it's a compulsion. I say it's insanity.

"Just a second!" I yelled down irritably.

Grub's ready. I hate when Dad says that. Believe me, grub in our house is true *grub*. Nothing edible is served here. Besides, it was just like my parents to interrupt my work— and right when I was on a roll.

I glared in the direction of the stairs, as if Mom and Dad were standing on the landing with their wheat-germ muffins and scrambled tofu with fig sauce in hand. Their idea of eating breakfast together on Saturday mornings has always gotten on my nerves, but this summer it was bugging me extra good.

I got up, stretched, and involuntarily let out a yelp that sounded like the bark of Mr. Conrad's toy poodle. I went over to the full-length mirror on the back of my door and examined myself carefully. My hair was sticking up every way possible but I left it alone. No sense trying to mat it down just to eat grub with Mom and Dad.

I walked over to the fishtank and sprinkled some goldfish food into the water. Mark Twain, Isaac Asimov, and Dashiell Hammett swam to the surface, lapping up the food hurriedly, their mouths making tiny Os. It was at times like these that I needed my famous-writer-inspired fish to inspire me. But they didn't.

Sighing again, I dragged my body down the stairs and into the kitchen, getting angrier with each step.

"You know, I've been thinking," I said as I took a seat at the table. "I may be outgrowing Saturday morning breakfasts. After all, I'll be in high school next fall. I think we should reconsider its place in the family routine."

"Lighten up, Jackie," Dad replied, stirring his coffee. "Have a muffin." Though both my parents are committed to "healthful eating," Dad has a severe weakness for coffee, which he drinks black. I've never understood why he stirs it, since he never adds anything. Another compulsion, I guess.

I made a face as he passed me a plate of his infamous, deformed-looking, sawdust-tasting wheat-germ muffins. I might as well have been performing for my goldfish, though, because Dad didn't look at me. I passed the plate back to him, muffins intact.

Have a muffin, he says. That was Dad's answer to everything. Well, it wasn't going to do the trick this time. It might have worked when I was ten or eleven, but now that I was thirteen, I knew better. And I knew what I wanted. I had sworn a blood oath on the lives of my goldfish that by the end of the summer I'd have written the great American novel. I had wanted to be a writer since I was five years old. Writing was what I loved. I was great at it, in fact.

As if reading my mind, Dad turned to me and said, "Are you thinking about your great American novel again?"

I involuntarily clenched my fists but told myself to be cool.

Mom didn't seem to hear me or Dad. Before I could respond, she interrupted cheerfully. "We have great news for you," she said, pouring Chinese green tea into a little white cup.

My stomach muscles tensed as I waited to hear this so-called great news. I was sure it would be another diversion from my writing. Mom and Dad don't take my writing seriously. You'd think that being editors themselves, they would support me. But no.

"You're going to love this, Jackie," Dad said in a singsong voice that reminded me of story time in kindergarten. "We're sending you to the best computer camp in the state this summer."

A few seconds of silence followed. "What?!" I finally said, in a voice that sounded like a frog croak.

"Diamond Jubilee Computer Camp," Mom said, enunciating each word carefully. "You'll love it. Guaranteed." She grinned at me. "If you do well, we'll even buy you a computer," she added in a playful tone.

I made a face. I didn't want a computer and I didn't want to go to Diamond Jubilee Computer Camp. I bet this camp started on Monday. They always sprang camp on me at the last minute—I should've known this summer would be no different.

Mom and Dad grinned at each other, then picked up their forks and started on the tofu. As far as they were concerned, the matter was closed. The only sound that followed was the clink of silverware against plates.

"Jackie, dear," Mom said, smiling gently, "your tofu's getting cold."

Well, as far as I was concerned, this summer I wasn't going to let them do it. "I am NOT going to computer camp," I said fiercely, rising from my chair in slow motion. "I'm not going to any kind of camp! Last year it was science camp, the year before it was tennis camp. No . . . more . . . camps! I'm staying in my room all summer and writing my novel!"

Both of them stared at me wordlessly, their forks frozen in midair.

"And I don't want any muffins—or tofu!"

With that, I stormed out.

Chapter 2

" It wasn't so much the blood that
bothered me as all the dead iguanas. **"**

Film noir is a lot of fun to write. Hard-boiled detective
meets beautiful client and terrible betrayal occurs. I got
excited by the mere thought of it. Maybe a movie studio
would pay millions of dollars to buy it, and I would be rich.
The more I thought about it, the more I knew film noir was
the answer.

I thought hard for several minutes, but it happened
again. I couldn't think of a sentence to follow my great
opening line. I looked desperately to my fish, but again they
disappointed me.

Well, at least I didn't have to eat breakfast with my parents
this morning. Mom and Dad said they were sorry about
Diamond Jubilee Computer Camp last Saturday. They said

they didn't know I really meant it this time. This time? What did they mean by that?

"Well," Dad replied, "last year you said you were going to write a short story about a psychopath, but . . ." He let his words trail off suggestively.

I was furious. So I didn't write that short story. Big deal. It wasn't my fault. It was theirs. They sent me to camp just as I was finishing it. Or starting it. Whatever. Anyway, that was the point. If I didn't go to camp, I'd have all the time in the world to write my novel.

I got up and stretched. It had taken me three hours to write my opening line. That was a significant improvement from one week. But I needed a break now. I needed to talk to someone who understood. Which meant only one thing. Mallory.

I grabbed the sheet of paper with my great opening line. Then I dressed in the clothes that were on top of my pile on the floor. As I headed for the stairs, I thought maybe I should start paying more attention to what I wore—now that I was going to be a famous, rich author. I looked down at what I had carelessly chosen to wear today. Wrinkled blue shorts and a baggy T-shirt that said, "Virginia Is for Lovers." I snorted. Did the T-shirt belong to me? Where had it come from? I would have to change. I couldn't go out in a T-shirt that said, "Virginia Is for Lovers."

I often thought about hanging up all my clothes, which had existed in a wrinkled pile on my floor for the last few years. Mom was always on my case about it. She said she wouldn't be surprised to find a family of vagrants living under it. When I reached the downstairs landing, still thinking about my clothes, I automatically stopped and took a quick look around before proceeding into the kitchen. Making sure there are no weirdos in the house is as basic to me as brushing my teeth. That's because my parents aren't normal. In fact, I cannot remember a time when they were ever normal. Even before they started their own publishing company, they were into yoga, meditation, organically grown produce, vitamins, herbs, tonics, and syrups with strange names.

But with Good for You Press around, things get weirder every day. My parents publish books about nutrition, fitness, meditation, alternative medicine, and spirituality. Their offices are in our house, and, for that reason, there is a stream of very strange people coming through here all the time. By strange, I mean *strange*. Not just women with half green and half purple hair—though one of their best-selling authors has half green and half purple hair—but men with tattoos of penguins on their arms and women who say, "The body knows" in every other sentence, such as "It's going to rain today. The body knows." Or, "Jackie, you've really grown. The body knows." And, "I think I'll watch TV tonight. The body knows."

Sometimes I wonder if I'm adopted. Actually, I was born in India. My parents were in the Peace Corps there. They say living in India changed their lives. I guess it changed mine, too. Maybe we should have stayed in India, where everyone meditates and drinks tea and has friends who say, "The body knows." Here in the United States of America, it's a little hard to fit in when you've got parents who do that. Believe me, I know. When I get rich and famous, the first thing I'm going to do is get my own place. With that thought in mind, I dialed Mallory's number.

The phone rang three times before she picked up. "Hello, your Theme Park Headquarters."

"Hey, it's me."

"Hey."

"You doing anything right now?"

"Nothing special."

"Wanna come over?"

"Sure. I'll be right over, m.p."

I hung up and smiled to myself. I knew I could count on Mallory.

Mallory Thompson is my best friend in the whole world. We have been friends since nursery school, when she toddled over to me and asked if I wanted to watch while she stuck a fat carrot up her nose. Naturally, I said yes. Later, we bonded in the emergency room.

Although Mallory is a girl and I'm not, she is the coolest person I know. Girls don't pay me much attention, and that's fine with me. Mallory is more like a boy anyway. Mom and Dad think it's "beneficial" that my best friend is a girl. They say it will be "fascinating" to see how our relationship changes as we "enter our teen years." I don't think anything is going to change. Mallory and I will always be best friends. Plus, she is the only person who really understands me. Even if she is some kind of theme-park freak.

Theme parks are Mallory's life. She's a walking theme-park encyclopedia. You could ask her, "When was Disneyland built?" and she'd tell you. You could ask, "How many theme parks are there in Texas?" and she'd know. You could say, "Which theme parks have animal safaris?" and she'd list them. Mallory is obsessed with theme parks. When she grows up, she wants to be a theme-park designer.

Ten minutes later, Mallory showed up at my door. "Hey," she mumbled, striding past me and into the kitchen.

I followed her, watching as she emptied the contents of our refrigerator onto the kitchen counter. "Any leftover muffins? I'm s.h.i.c.e.a.h."

"No," I replied impatiently. Mallory spoke in abbreviations. I could never figure out why. What she meant was "I'm so hungry I could eat a horse." I watched as she picked through our fruits and vegetables and finally selected an organically grown papaya from the island of Maui.

"So," she said, taking a seat at the kitchen table with her papaya and a knife. "What's up, m.p.?" (My pal.)

"Well," I said, joining her at the table. "I got out of going to Diamond Jubilee Computer Camp. You know, the one I told you about."

"Mah-velous," she said, carefully slicing the papaya in half.

"I need the time to write," I added, in case Mallory had forgotten that part.

"Mmmm-hmmm," she replied absently, sniffing the papaya's orange interior.

"I'm having a little trouble though," I went on.

"Uh-huh," she said, meticulously scraping the seeds out of the papaya into a bowl.

"I need inspiration," I continued, growing annoyed.

"Right."

"Are you listening to me?"

"Sure, m.p. Let me see what you've got so far," she replied, poking the papaya with one hand and holding out her other hand to me.

Reluctantly, I handed her the sheet of paper. Mallory was the only person in the world I ever showed my writing-in-progress to, except teachers.

She read it silently. "Why are the iguanas dead?" she finally asked after a few minutes.

"That's not the point," I said, slightly peeved. I was really proud of the iguana part.

"Man, this is great papaya," she said, holding out a papaya piece to me.

"Mallory! Will you forget the stupid papaya!"

"But I've got it!" she said excitedly. "Listen to this, m.p. Why don't you write a novel about a t.p. in Illinois, and all the *intrigues* that happen there." (Theme park.) She emphasized the word "intrigues," then shoved three papaya cubes into her mouth in quick succession. She looked at me, chewing triumphantly.

I gave her a long look. "I'm surrounded by lunatics," I said.

"Hey!" she replied, sounding hurt. "That's a great idea."

"That's because *you* love theme parks." I pointed at her, then folded my arms in frustration and sat back in my chair.

She shrugged. It was her constant response when pressed.

I gave a loud sigh.

"Why don't you ask your parents for help?"

"No way!" I cried, throwing my arms up. "They're too weird. They don't know anything."

"But they do this for a living. I bet they'd know what to do."

"Forget it," I said and meant it.

"Well, maybe you should hang out more with your friends, observe them, get ideas."

"Friends? What has that got to do with this?"

Before she could answer, the doorbell rang. I looked out the window to see Garus and Nick milling around aimlessly on our front porch in their bathing suits.

"Aha," Mallory chirped. "Your friends have arrived, just as I predicted." She shoved three more papaya cubes into her mouth and smiled at me with bloated cheeks.

I was not amused. Nick and Garus were the last thing I needed right now. They were my friends, but all they ever wanted to do were stupid things. I really needed to work on my novel. I couldn't ignore them, though, because they had already seen us through the window. Nick gave a slight wave.

I groaned and got up to go to the door. "Hey, guys," I said nervously, opening the door a crack.

"Mallory, babe," Nick said, peering behind me. "How's life on Theme Park Planet?"

"Get out of my face, loser," Mallory responded cheerfully.

Nick looked genuinely hurt. But he was always asking for it. He fancied himself a ladies' man. Mallory was sort of a safe target, so he practiced his "babe lines"—as he called them—on her. And failed.

"Funny girl," he muttered, getting his comb out of his pocket and combing his already combed hair.

Garus gazed up at Nick adoringly. Garus was a joke. He used a lot of big words delivered in a pseudo-English accent, and was always doing Nick's bidding. His real name was Gary, but a long time ago Nick christened him "Garus," because "Gary" wasn't a "real name." Since Nick was really Nicholas and I was really John, Gary had to be something more, too. Besides, Nick said, Garus suited him, since it implied "a dignified British gentleman." I had to laugh at that one. Nobody, especially Nick, thought Garus was dignified or British or a gentleman.

I guess Nick and Garus had what my science teacher would call a "symbiotic relationship." Garus needed to be around someone cooler than he was, and Nick needed someone to think he was the coolest guy ever.

"Jackie, old bean," Garus said, turning to me. "By the bye, we are here to inform you that we are joining the swim team tomorrow."

"Sorry, Garus. Did I hear you say something about 'we' and 'join' and 'tomorrow'?" I said.

"Are you cooped up in your room with your stupid typewriter again?" Nick asked, getting right to the point.

"Uh . . . no." I shuffled my feet self-consciously. I was never much of a liar. I wish I could be. But I wasn't.

They looked at each other and smirked, then turned back to me. "Listen, Mr. Great Writer," Nick said in stuffy tones, "Mr. Arnold Hemingway."

"Ernest," I said.

"Whatever. We need you on the swim team." He took a small mirror out of his pocket and checked his hair in it.

"I'm sorry, guys," I stammered. "I can't."

Even as I refused, a part of me hoped they would ask again. I loved swimming. Swimming, in fact, came as easily to me as writing.

"Jackie," Mallory piped up from behind me. "Go on!"

I looked over at her. She was smiling again with bloated cheeks. I wondered if it was a new round of papaya cubes in her mouth or the same ones I had last seen.

"Well . . ." I stalled.

"You wanted my help, right?" Mallory went on, her voice muffled because of the papaya. "I think it would be good for you to join the swim team. You could get a lot of material from it."

She got up, still chewing, and walked to the doorway where we all stood.

"It would do you good, old chap," Garus said. "Be like a holiday."

"Listen to the little lady," Nick said. As fast as lightning, Mallory's fist went out and punched him in the shoulder. Nick stepped back, then looked at her with surprise. "That hurt, baby," he said, rubbing his shoulder. Garus glared at Mallory contemptuously, but she ignored him.

Mallory was a little on the short side, and anytime anyone ever referred to her as "little" or "small" or "short," they got a sock in response. I once made the mistake of calling her "petite," and she punched me right in the nose. It bled for twenty-five minutes.

"As we were saying before we were so rudely interrupted," Garus continued, casting a sidelong glance at Mallory, "will you join us, old boy?"

I looked longingly up the stairs toward my room. I did want to swim, but I needed to write. I turned back to my friends. Garus and Nick were studying me closely.

"Oh, all right," I relented. "I know I'm going to regret this."

"That's what they all say," Mallory said, then headed back to her papaya.

Chapter 3

“In the year 2074, the human race finally
defeated the X-Jowls in their long battle
for domination of the universe,
but the real war was just beginning.”

Forget film noir. What I really wanted to write was science fiction. *The Terminator* meets *Star Wars*. I would be the next George Lucas!

I hunched over the typewriter, my mind racing with possibilities—X-Jowl versus human, man versus woman, dog versus cat.

One minute went by, then two minutes went by, then three. I swallowed back the sudden panic that began to swirl in the pit of my stomach. "Let's see," I said nervously. "What should happen next? The leader of the X-Jowls arrives? The space army meets for a briefing? The beautiful spy Warsha-Y receives her lethal orders?"

Three more minutes went by. Sighing, I pressed my hands onto the keys. The result was "hfffbhbffkccvcfjfjfj-dsfhfgr." And then the doorbell rang.

Reluctantly, I got up. "I shall return," I told the type-writer menacingly. I backed out of the room, crouching *Mission Impossible* style. "Don't go anywhere," I warned the machine, pointing my finger.

Satisfied that I had sufficiently intimidated my type-writer into cooperating, I joined Nick and Garus on the front porch. Nick was winking at himself in the mirror, first with his right eye, then with his left, while Garus watched in fascination, hoping to learn something.

"Why, Hemingway, you've come to grace us with your presence?" Nick asked, putting the mirror away quickly.

"Your intuition is astounding," I said, shutting the door behind me.

"Thanks," Nick said, his face brightening at the seeming compliment. He punched me in the arm lightly. "You won't regret this."

I snorted. I was *already* regretting it. The last thing I needed was a distraction, especially since I had managed to get rid of camp.

Mr. Conrad and his toy poodle, Fifi, were standing on the corner, as if waiting for us to arrive. When she saw us approaching, Fifi began to yelp happily. Nick instinctively started to cross the street, but I put my hand on his arm to stop him. "Fifi wouldn't hurt a fly," I told him.

Nick's eyes darted wildly from her to me. He was deathly afraid of dogs. When he was just a baby, a dog the size of a sperm whale nearly bit off his hand. He still has the scar.

"You sure, Hemingway?" he asked in a shaky voice.

Garus looked at me with the same wariness, concern for his hero overshadowing his love for dogs. He had three golden retrievers at home and was always shoving them into the laundry room when Nick came over.

"I'm positive," I said confidently.

Nick followed behind me tentatively, taking baby steps forward. Garus, his brow furrowed in concentration, walked behind Nick.

"Hi, Mr. Conrad," I said when we reached the corner.

"Hello, boys," he replied pleasantly. "Such a beautiful day. Going swimming?"

I nodded. Mr. Conrad was a kindly old man with white hair that stuck out all over his head. He looked like Albert Einstein. He lived alone in a house on the next block and rarely left it except to walk Fifi.

I reached down to pet Fifi. Her tail wagged crazily when my hand made contact with her. She licked my fingers in long, wet slops. Garus, temporarily overcome by his love for dogs, got down on his knees in front of her. Fifi stood on her hind legs and put her paws around his neck. She licked his face and Garus giggled like he was a little kid.

I felt as though we had all been transported into a Kodak commercial, until Fifi laid eyes on Nick. He was standing apart from the rest of us, looking like he was ready to bolt. Fifi regarded him silently, then a menacing growl escaped from deep in her throat. She growled again, bared her teeth, and, before we could stop her, charged Nick.

Nick let out a shriek and took off. Luckily, Fifi was on a leash. As soon as she reached the end of it, she bounced back toward Mr. Conrad like a rubber band.

"My goodness," Mr. Conrad said, staring at his dog with a mixture of shock and amusement. "What in the world was that about?" He picked up Fifi and petted her.

"Nick doesn't like dogs," I ventured.

"He was bitten by one of our canine friends when he was just a young infant," Garus said soberly.

Mr. Conrad looked at Garus. "Where do you hail from?" he asked.

Garus's eyes widened with pleasure. "London." He glanced at me quickly. "My ancestors," he added.

Mr. Conrad nodded. Fifi was squirming in his arms. "Well, I better get her home," he said. He put her down gently on the sidewalk. Fifi immediately struggled against her leash in the direction that Nick had run. Mr. Conrad watched her for a few seconds, then pulled her toward his house.

Nick was a speck in the distance. By the time we caught up with him, he was a cool guy again, leaning against a telephone pole, scowling at nothing in particular.

"Hey, guys," he said casually.

"Hey," we answered automatically. Even though we had seen Nick run, scared for his life, with our own eyes, it was not mentioned again. We walked silently until we reached the swim club, and by then I had gone back to worrying about my novel.

The Frog Hollow Swim Club is one of those self-contained entities cut off from the rest of the planet. When you enter its hallowed gates, you enter a world with its own laws.

The first thing you see is a gathering of people around the front desk, a.k.a. the Lifeguard Command Center, where everyone checks in and the first-aid equipment gathers mold. Garus was doing his best to imitate Nick's cool-guy walk as he passed them, but it was impossible in the neon green bathing suit he was wearing. I briefly considered telling him how stupid he looked, but Garus is sensitive about his taste, so I didn't.

Nick was waltzing around in his I'm-a-macho-guy stride, the kind of walk he uses when he's trying to impress girls. Nick believes it is his birthright to have beautiful girls on his arm, which, of course, has never actually happened. I don't know who put this notion into his head. He had a girlfriend named Caroline once for three days, and it was a disaster. He brought her to his family's Fourth of July picnic, and she made lasagna. Unfortunately, Nick's family is known for making great Italian food, something he forgot to tell Caroline. Her lasagna was joined on the picnic table by two other lasagnas, two chicken parmigianas, four manicottis, and two trays of ravioli. Not only did the Positano family decide that Caroline's lasagna tasted like dog food, but they decided right in front of her, by a vote of 17 to 1 (that was Nick voting against). Caroline left the picnic in tears, and Nick never saw her again.

I'm sure Nick was going over this sad episode in his head when we passed a group of girls in bikinis. He fidgeted nervously, and I could see him trying to decide whether or not to snatch a quick look in his mirror. After several seconds, he decided no.

A hand-lettered sign past the snack bar read "Swim Team—Line Up At Pool." About twelve other boys were already there, standing motionlessly at the pool's edge and watching the water as if it were a TV screen.

The girls in bikinis giggled as Nick, Garus, and I joined the others with grim expressions on our faces. I snuck a glance at one of the bikini girls and saw her staring at me. Quickly, I looked away, but not before I saw her smile. A strange feeling came over me, making me warm all over.

I was beginning to think this might not be so bad after all. Then a guy came out of nowhere and stood in front of us. He held a banana in one hand and a stopwatch in the other. A silver whistle hung around his neck. He fingered the whistle, as if considering whether or not to use it, and ultimately decided he would. He brought it to his lips and blew so hard I thought I'd soon be deaf.

"Listen up!" he boomed. "I'm the coach!" Then he proceeded to tell us, "No one is too good to get kicked off this team!" At which point he screamed, "If you don't want to work, you might as well quit now!"

I was contemplating that option precisely when he shouted, "Move it! Move it!"

The sound of bodies splashing into the water startled me, and I realized we were supposed to do laps. I dove into the chilly water along with Nick and Garus and swam for my life. I did about twenty laps before I noticed I was the only one left in the water. By the time I hauled my carcass out of the pool I was ready to pass out right there on the concrete.

"I want to see everyone in the diving area now!" Coach screeched before any of us could get our hands on towels. Dripping and cold, I hurried to the diving area, only to be met by an earsplitting whistle. "I said NOW, you lowlifes!" he shrieked, looking right at me.

I lined up quickly next to Nick and stood there shivering,

wondering why in the world I had decided to join the swim team.

Coach paced up and down silently in front of our line as if he were a general surveying his troops. He stopped in front of me. "You listening, boy?" he asked menacingly.

"Yes," I said, in a voice that sounded strange to me.

"Good," he replied. He pointed his banana at me, then began peeling it in swift strokes, all the time keeping his eyes on me.

"You swim like clumsy tadpoles," he announced, chomping the banana so fiercely it made me wince. He walked back down the line, studying each of us in turn.

"I'm going to turn you into sleek sharks," he said, and if it had been anyone else, I would have laughed. I'd never seen anyone who could make eating a banana seem so scary.

He stopped abruptly, holding out the banana peel in one hand. A kid suddenly came out of nowhere and relieved Coach of it, spiriting it away to an unknown trash can reserved for such things.

Coach put his hands behind his back. "We've got some talent here," he said. "Some real talent." He didn't look at me as he said this.

"But we've got to refine it," he continued, raising a fist in the air. "We've got to perfect it." He shook his fist three times. "You tadpoles are going to have to *earn* your meets. I'm not scheduling any until you do. You understand?" he asked in a low voice.

Nobody answered.

"I said, you understand?" he asked more loudly.

Several boys nodded. One kid said, "Yeah."

Coach glanced at him, nodding. "When I say you under-

24

stand, I want to hear that you understand," he said. "You understand?"

We all shouted, "Yes!" in unison. Coach seemed surprised but recovered quickly. "Good," he said, clapping his hands together twice. "Then let's do some real swimming. When I call your name, dive in, do four laps, get out, fill out this form, come back tomorrow. Got it?"

My mind was struggling to process all this information when the bikini girl reappeared.

She smiled at me—right at me—and I found myself smiling back. I was thinking how beautiful she was when it occurred to me that something was terribly wrong. All the other boys were staring at me. Nick looked so scared I thought he was going to die.

Coach glared at me. "Are you having a problem, boy?" he asked.

"No," I whispered. I realized that while I was smiling at the bikini girl Coach had called my name, but instead of diving into the pool and doing my laps I had stood there with a stupid smile on my face.

Coach walked right up to me, his face inches from mine. "I don't need any problems, boy. You understand?" He didn't wait for me to answer. "You got problems in mind, you better leave now. Otherwise, you swim. That's what we're all here to do. Swim. You ready to swim, boy?"

I nodded.

"Too bad. You lost your turn." He turned his back to me and called Garus, who instantly jumped into the water. The bikini girl disappeared.

I stood there for the next hour as each boy did his laps. Finally, Coach called "Monterey" just like that, and I did my laps. I was so tired from standing up for so long that I could hardly get my legs to work. Coach watched me steadily but said nothing.

When I got out of the pool, Nick and Garus were already at the snack bar, chomping on cheeseburgers that looked a little overdone. The bikini girls were at a nearby table, sharing a bucket of French fries.

"Hey," I said, sitting down next to Nick.

Nick smiled, bits of cheese clinging to his teeth. He gestured to the girls. "I think one of those chicks likes you, Hemingway."

I followed his gaze and saw the beautiful girl. She was putting a French fry in her mouth, and it occurred to me that no one had ever eaten a French fry in a more adorable way. She saw me looking at her and smiled shyly.

"Gentlemen," Garus said, clearing his throat self-consciously. "By the bye, I have reason to believe there is, well, a problem of sorts with this young lady."

Nick took another bite. "What are you talking about?" he asked.

Garus pointed at Coach, who was talking to a lifeguard. His back was turned to us, and we could see "Phillips" clearly written on the back of his swim-team jacket.

"So?" I asked.

Just then, the girls got up. The air had gotten cooler and they pulled their jackets on in a clamor of giggles. The beautiful girl gave me a parting smile, then turned to go with her friends. Her jacket, which was identical to Coach's, said "Phillips," too, and as if any more evidence was needed, she kissed Coach on the cheek as she passed him.

"Bye, Dad," she called sweetly.

Chapter 4

" So I said, 'I'll take the good
news,' and that was my first mistake. **"**

Forget science fiction. Film noir it was going to be. And
this time it would work. I just needed a good name for my
main character before I could write more. Then I would
definitely get past the opening line.

I was sitting on the couch in the living room, flipping
through the baby-naming tome my parents published every
year—*Spiritual Names for Your Precious Gift*—trying to find
a really great name. It wasn't that I wanted a spiritual name
for my hard-boiled detective, but I had already tried the
telephone book and come up with nothing—I guess people
in our town don't have very exciting names.

As I browsed through the book, I groaned every now and
then.

Stormy. Groan.

Spirit. Groan.

Divine Wonder. Groan.

My body was completely mangled from the week of swimming practice we'd had, and the groaning helped a little. Mallory sat next to me on the couch, twirling her hair and reading the latest issue of *Theme Park Executive*.

"How's the swim team, m.p.?" she asked after my sixth groan.

"It stinks," I said. "Coach is a complete jerk. I'm a great swimmer, but he keeps telling us we're bad. I don't need any help with swimming. I wish he'd leave me alone."

"Maybe he doesn't think you're such a great swimmer," she replied casually, not looking up from her magazine.

I glowered at Mallory, but she kept reading.

"I'm a *great* swimmer," I said, trying to sound as convincing as I could.

Mallory glanced up at me. "Maybe he can make you better," she said, then turned back to her magazine again.

"But I'm fine the way I am," I said, my voice suddenly sounding whiny. I cleared my throat. "Swimming and writing are the things I'm best at," I said confidently.

"Sometimes people know that they could be better, but they won't admit it," she said. "They pretend everything's fine."

I tried to think of a clever reply, but instead I said, "Let's just drop it, O.K.?"

"O.K., p.s.s.," she chirped. (Poor sore swimmer, her latest pet name for me.)

I turned back to the naming book, putting Mallory's comments out of my head. Swimming and writing were the two things I was best at. End of story.

Besides, I had my own theory as to why Coach was so hard on me, and it revolved around two words: Kelly Phillips. My face involuntarily broke into a smile when I thought of her. I still hadn't gotten up the nerve to actually talk to her, but I looked forward to practice every day just to be able to see her, and when she wasn't there, I felt strangely disappointed.

Nick was too busy chasing one of Kelly's girlfriends to notice my crush, and Garus was too busy watching Nick—hoping to learn something—so I was pretty much on my own when it came to Kelly. Except for Coach, that is. He was watching me closely, and I knew it.

"How's your novel going?" Mallory asked, disrupting my thoughts.

"Great," I said quickly. "I just need a good name for my main character." All of this was true, I told myself, feeling annoyed for having to do that.

"I've got an amazing name for you," Mallory said with a sparkle in her eyes.

"What?" I asked curiously.

"George Ferris!"

I grimaced. "George Ferris?"

"Yeah, he invented the Ferris wheel!" she cried excitedly, clasping her hands together and smiling.

I shook my head and turned back to my book. "I don't think so, Mallory," I said.

Mallory studied me for a long time in silence, until I had to look up. "What?" I asked crossly.

"I'll tell you what your problem is, m.p.," she said, the words tumbling out rapidly. "You think you can do this all by yourself. Locked away in your room. But the truth is, you can't. You need help. Advice. Like swimming." She turned back to her magazine as if she had said nothing important.

I was about to ask her what she meant by "like swimming" as well as tell her that I did NOT need anyone's help. But she suddenly let out a long shriek.

"What?" I demanded.

"Will you look at this!" she ordered, thrusting the magazine in my face.

"'First Annual Young Writers Competition,'" I read aloud. "'Grand prize is a fabulous all-inclusive trip for you and up to five guests to Kingdom of Magic.'"

Mallory pulled the magazine away from me and read the rest. "'The grand-prize winner will also receive a special VIP tour and meet with officials of our magical theme park.'"

I peered at her with what must have been confusion in my eyes. "So?" I asked.

Mallory looked at me quizzically. "So?!" she repeated. "I . . . CAN'T . . . BELIEVE . . . THIS!" she hollered at the top of her lungs.

"Mallory, stop it!" I yelled impatiently. "You're acting like a lunatic."

"Don't you know what this means, m.p.?" she asked. "This," she indicated the magazine, "is the opportunity I've been waiting for." She sighed loudly. "'Special VIP tour and meet with officials of our magical theme park,'" she mumbled, and then I realized that for Mallory seeing how a theme park works would be the equivalent of my getting a novel published.

"I'm so happy I could cry," she said, hugging the magazine to her chest.

And with that, she started sobbing.

Chapter 5

> Cal Lee Troy pushed back his cowboy hat and wiped the heavy sweat off his brow. He skimmed the vast grasslands slowly, his eyes coming to rest upon a strange black shape in the distance.

A Western is definitely the way to go. Who needs film noir?

"Jackie! Dinner!"

"Just a minute!" I called back, eager to get down a few more sentences.

"Jackie!" Dad called again. "We're all waiting!"

I looked at my watch. Six o'clock—on the dot.

"One second!" But the momentum was broken. My mind was mush.

I sighed. "They did it to me again," I said under my breath. I studied Mark, Isaac, and Dashiell. "Guys, this is harder than I thought," I confessed, then got up and headed downstairs.

Mom, Dad, and Mallory, our guest for the evening, were seated around the table. Mallory loved being invited for dinner at our house. She said my parents' healthful cooking was so g.f.y. (Good for you.)

"I don't agree," I once told her.

"Why not?" she asked indignantly.

"I'm not especially fond of soy yogurt with elderberry sauce," I said in my most sarcastic voice.

Mallory rolled her eyes. "Just because your parents don't sink their teeth into T-bone steaks doesn't mean the food they eat is strange."

"Do you live with them or do I?" I asked, then realized I was being a little too obnoxious. But Mallory had decided to ignore my comment anyway.

When I sat down at the dinner table, I knew Mallory was wrong—this food *was* strange.

"Creamed ginger root, Mallory?" Dad asked, as if he were offering chocolate cake with whipped cream.

"Oh, yes," Mallory sang out, with an equal amount of enthusiasm.

"Oat-bran roll?" Dad offered, glad to have someone at the table besides Mom who appreciated his cooking.

"Mmmm, yes," Mallory replied, as if she had been given precious stones.

I looked at her plate overflowing with Mom and Dad's idea of dinner and shook my head. How could she eat it? My own plate contained a microscopic amount of collard greens with pine nuts and a crumb of an oat-bran roll.

My parents smiled at Mallory. I knew they wished I were more like her. I knew they loved the fact that she indulged their strange ways. I knew they felt she would one day grow up and be the kind of person who ate tofu and drank Chinese green tea. She had it in her already. She was o.o.t. (One of them.)

Mallory was shoving food into her mouth and chattering a mile a minute about her writing competition. "I started it yesterday," she gushed with a mouth full of ginger. "I worked on it all day!"

"What's the topic of the essay?" Mom asked between delicate bites of collard greens.

"How I Spent My Summer Vacation," Mallory said, then frowned to show her displeasure.

Mom made a sympathetic noise. "Why, you haven't even had your whole summer vacation yet!" she said. "What are you going to write about?"

Mallory gave a quick flick of her wrist. "It doesn't have to be about this summer vacation. It can be about any summer vacation."

Mom nodded thoughtfully. I could tell she was thinking of what she might write if she were in Mallory's shoes. Mom often did that with her authors—put herself in their place. She said it made her a better editor.

"I really admire your determination, Mallory," Dad said. "I know how hard it is to complete a writing project."

I glanced up, a funny feeling in my stomach, or was it the ginger?

"Writing is very difficult," he continued. "I have the utmost respect for writers. When they finish what they start."

I looked at my plate. I tangled collard greens between the tines of my fork, studying the mess it made.

Mallory nodded in agreement. "It's really hard. I'm all alone—just me and the computer—trying to fill a bunch of blank pages."

I looked over and felt a sudden kinship with her at that moment. I'd never heard anyone describe the writing process that way, and yet, that was exactly how it felt. Except that I used a typewriter instead of a computer. I could have used a computer. Mom and Dad had two in their office, but I stayed away from there as much as possible. Besides, all the great writers had used typewriters. And that's what I wanted to be, a great writer.

"I really admire anyone who writes for a living," Dad went on.

Something—I don't know what—made me blurt out, "I write for a living." I instantly regretted it.

Three faces turned to me in surprise. There was total silence for about ten seconds.

"Um," Mom said, "I think what your father was referring to was professional writers."

"I'm a professional writer," I insisted, then wondered why I said that.

They were all silent again. Then Mom asked, "Well, how is *your* novel going?"

"Uh, really good," I answered uncomfortably. "Really, really good."

"Have you written a lot?"

"Uh, not exactly," I stammered. "But, it's going really well. Yeah, really well. Great, in fact."

"What kind of novel is it?" Mom asked, in a voice she used with her authors.

"Western," I said in a small voice.

"Who's the main character?"

"Cal Lee Troy," I said, proud of his authentic-sounding name.

"Good name," Dad said.

"What's the plot?" Mom continued, all business now.

"Well," I said, feeling uneasy now that I was the center of attention. "He's a cowboy. He has a ranch, see. And, uh, bandits are stealing his cattle."

Everyone nodded politely, so I went on. "So he fights them, see," I muttered. "And, uh, he gets his cattle back. But, I don't know the ending yet. Uh, but that's what I have so far."

"Sounds interesting," Mom said, and I wondered if she meant it.

"Yeah," I said blankly. Now that I had actually shared my novel with my parents—which I had not planned to do—I felt like I had to tell them the truth. "Uh, you know . . . ," I began awkwardly.

Mom turned to me, still in editor mode. "Yes?"

"Well, my novel is going really well—really, really well. But I'm having a little trouble with it, you know?"

"What kind of trouble?"

I noticed that Mallory was watching me with fascination and wondered what she was thinking.

"Well, I'm having trouble with the story, see," I said. "I can think of a great opening line. Really great. Fantastic, even. But the rest of it . . . well, it's hard."

I wiped my sweaty palms on my napkin, hoping they were getting the gist of what I was saying. That for the past few weeks I couldn't write more than opening lines.

"Have you read a lot of Westerns?" Dad asked abruptly.

"Uh, no," I said, shifting nervously in my seat, puzzled as to what he was getting at.

"The thing is," he said, putting his fork down and giving me his full attention, "you need *experience* to tell a story. For example, with a Western, you need to have been a cowboy yourself, or read about them, or done research on them."

I found myself nodding, wanting Dad to go on.

"Or," he continued, "you need imagination. To write science fiction, for instance."

He paused. I realized I had been holding my breath.

"Not everyone has an active imagination," Dad said. "Although that can sometimes be developed."

"Look at James Michener," Mom piped in. "He served in the South Pacific during World War II, so he wrote *Tales of the South Pacific* when he returned to the States. Or Michael Crichton. Or John Grisham. Crichton was once a doctor, so a lot of his books are medical- and science-related, while Grisham, who is a lawyer, writes about law."

"Write what you know," Dad said, emphasizing the words.

"On the other hand," Mom went on, "Stephen King has quite an imagination. He tells stories none of us could ever think of. And they're not based on any experience."

"We hope," Dad said, and they all laughed and then looked at me expectantly.

"I don't understand, uh, how this applies to me," I said.

"Write what you know," Dad repeated.

"Oh," I said, not having a clue. "I see."

Mallory grinned at me, apparently pleased that I had finally allowed my parents to give me advice. But I honestly had no idea what they were talking about. Write what I know? What did I know? Certainly not anything that would make a good novel.

I decided to ignore the rest of the conversation and concentrate on eating, and by the end of the meal, I had resolved to go back to my Western.

Chapter 6

"Professor Sanford Herringbone skillfully hacked at the dense jungle growth as his guide Faka Kulu pointed to the small village ahead. 'We must be careful,' he warned."

My cowboy Cal Lee Troy had ridden off into the sunset, abandoning me and his cattle. But Professor Sanford Herringbone and Faka Kulu showed up instead. I'd always wanted to write an adventure story—headhunters, buried treasure, malaria. The only problem was, I couldn't come up with anything else for my two main characters to do.

"You got any ideas, guys?" I asked my goldfish.

Nothing. Just a lot of bubbles.

A kind of despair began to wash over me.

You might think I'd be ready to give up this whole novel business about now, right? Wrong. I have wanted to be a writer since I was in kindergarten with Mrs. Crabtree. Mrs.

Crabtree launched my writing career. She insisted that we kindergartners spend every Friday telling each other stories, which she wrote down and collected in a booklet at the end of the year. I always told the most imaginative ones. That's what Mrs. Crabtree said anyway. She predicted I'd be an important writer one day. Mrs. Crabtree was about ninety years old now and couldn't remember my name, much less her prediction, but I had sworn I'd dedicate my first novel to her.

I stared out the window at the backyard. Mom was working in the herb garden, whistling as she weeded. Dad stood nearby, watering and also whistling. I shook my head. Even the herbs they grew were weird. They couldn't grow basil and parsley like everyone else in Frog Hollow. No, they had to grow feverfew, echinacea, and kava.

I sighed. Last night after Mallory left I overheard them talking about my writing.

"He has great ideas," Mom had said. "But he never sticks with anything. He has no perseverance."

"He wants to be a writer pretty badly," Dad said.

Mom shrugged. "He has to finish something first."

I couldn't believe it! Saying I had no "perseverance." So I didn't write that short story last year. So I didn't finish that essay two years ago. This time I would finish—I would show them that I had the most "perseverance" of anyone they knew. This year, I was going to write and *finish* my novel.

The sound of the doorbell just then startled me out of my reverie. Pulling on a tattered bathrobe, I tiptoed downstairs.

Nick and Garus stood at the front door, both in battered hiking boots, looking sour. I blinked in the bright sunlight. "Hey, guys," I said.

Nick's eyes widened. "Did you just get up, man?"

I quickly glanced at my watch. Well, it *was* one o'clock in the afternoon. "Um, yeah," I said sheepishly.

"Having a lie-in, old boy?" Garus asked with delight.

Both Nick and I stared at him. "Never mind," he grumbled.

"Get dressed, Hemingway," Nick said. "We're going." He adjusted his pants. He was wearing the tightest jeans I'd ever seen on a human being.

"Where?" I asked, my curiosity getting the best of me.

"We're going to the woods behind my house, old chap," Garus replied. "Nick's brother says he saw a copy of *Playboy* there last month."

We all fell silent for a moment. Then I said, "You're going to the woods behind your house to hunt down the remains of a fossilized *Playboy?*"

Nick and Garus studied me blankly.

"You coming or not?" Nick finally said.

I thought it over. Maybe it wouldn't hurt to have a small distraction. I hated doing stupid things with Nick and Garus—which is all they ever did—but I wasn't getting much done anyway.

"O.K.," I answered.

Fifteen minutes later, the three of us were wandering around the woods behind Garus's house. "Examine every piece of paper you come across," Nick instructed us with the air of a pro. He was practically drooling.

I scowled at him, wondering why I agreed to go on this nature hike. Maybe being alone in my room with my typewriter wasn't so bad after all.

Crushing twigs and leaves underfoot with our heavy boots, we made our way stupidly through the dense trees.

Then the sunshine turned to clouds, and a light rain started to fall. I looked at Garus and grimaced. In vain, Nick tried to protect his hair. He made a useless motion to reach into his back pocket for his comb—but he couldn't get his hand inside his skintight jeans. I laughed.

Nick frowned at me. "Shut up, moron," he said lightly.

Suddenly, a few feet away, a piece of paper called out to us. We all dove at the same time, scrambling to get ahold of it.

"Hey, you jerk, I got it."

"No you don't."

"Let me in there."

Pretty soon the fight was over, and we all stood there, holding an ad for Tide with Bleach. "%#$@&!"

We continued on our muddy hike, the rain getting heavier and heavier. I looked up at the sky, and a big fat raindrop fell right into my eyeball. "%#$@&!"

We finally came to a stump in a small clearing. Inside the stump were several rotted pieces of paper. I bent down to pick up a branch and attempted to push them out, to no avail.

We each took turns with the branch. Finally, in desperation, Nick shoved his arm into the slimy interior of the stump and retrieved the paper.

We were awe-struck. We had found it! A few pages of a tattered copy of *Playboy*. But we soon discovered there were no pictures. We looked at it for a little while in a kind of dumb stupor, waiting for something to happen.

"Let's get out of here," Nick finally said.

We made our way to Garus's house. Nick and I waited

outside, getting more and more soaked, while Garus did his dog-clearing routine. Garus's mother peeked out the front door and peered at Nick and me. She shook her head, as if thinking, Why do these nice boys do such stupid things? At that moment, I wanted to tell her that I agreed with her.

"Would you like to come in for some hot cocoa?" she asked brightly.

Nick smiled gratefully and headed inside. Mrs. White looked at him threateningly as he approached the welcome mat. Thankfully, Nick remembered his manners and wiped his muddy boots carefully. Mrs. White smiled appreciatively. She then gazed at me expectantly.

"No, thank you," I said. "I'm going home." The last thing I needed was to do more stupid things today.

Garus's mother nodded. I could tell she was happy about only having to make two cocoas instead of three.

I trudged back to the house, shivering and miserable, but after I'd dried off and settled in front of my typewriter, Professor Sanford Herringbone and Faka Kulu did not visit again.

Chapter 7

"Divine Wonder made one last adjustment to her bunny ears. Then the Playboy-bunny-hopeful walked across the hall to see her boss, the mysterious Lady MacKenzie Greystone, who was waiting in an anteroom."

A novel about a Playboy bunny is ridiculous. But it was all I could think of after yesterday.

"This stinks," I said, ripping out the sheet of paper and crumpling it into a ball. It was Nick and Garus's fault. Dragging me on a rainy nature hike just when I was getting into Professor Sanford Herringbone and Faka Kulu.

Well, I was out of time anyway. Swim practice was starting soon, and I had to get ready. I put on my bathing suit and headed downstairs for a bite to eat. There was some leftover pizza in the fridge, so I unwrapped a slice, set it on a plate, and warmed it in the microwave.

My mom's pizza isn't as bad as some of the other foods she and Dad cook. Mom makes it with strange vegetables like Swiss chard and okra, but it has regular cheese and sauce on it, so it is edible.

The microwave beeped, and I carried the steaming slice of pizza to the table and sat down. As I ate the limp slice, I daydreamed about what it would be like to kiss Kelly Phillips. The most beautiful girl in Frog Hollow was at the swim club every day, but I still hadn't ever talked to her. Nick said I was avoiding her, and maybe I was. She was Coach's daughter, after all.

I looked at my watch and hurried out the door. The last time I was late, Coach made me do an extra six laps. When I got to the swim club, Nick and Garus were already in the water. Coach was busy chatting with one of the lifeguards, so I slipped into the pool quietly, hoping he wouldn't see me.

I had done about four laps when he called us all out. We lined up quickly at the pool's edge. We were used to lining up at the sound of his whistle while still wet and dripping now. None of us even brought towels anymore. In fact, when I took a shower the other day, I forgot to towel off. It was only after I got into my clothes that I realized I was still wet.

Thanks a lot, Coach.

Coach walked down the line studying each of us in turn. I swear that when he got to me he frowned. Then he looked away and walked back to the other end of the line.

"Boys, you're making real progress," he said. "Real progress indeed."

I thought I saw him smile, but I must have imagined it. Coach never smiled. He was quiet for several seconds, and then he dropped a bombshell on us.

"I think we're ready for our first meet," he said, and a huge gasp went up from everyone.

A meet! I couldn't believe it! We were actually going to compete against another team!

Coach eyed each of us slowly, as if determining our worthiness for such an important mission. "We'll be competing against Brewster," he added matter-of-factly, and everyone gasped again.

"Yikes," Nick said to me under his breath.

Brewster! Brewster was our mortal enemy. They were the next town over and always beat us in everything—football, baseball, hockey, soccer, tennis. Everyone who lived in Frog Hollow wanted to beat everyone who lived in Brewster at some sport. The only problem was, they were too good. The last time we had beaten Brewster was in 1968 in a baseball game. We had lost to them every year since then. Our baseball team in particular was ashamed of itself.

"Boys," Coach went on, "I don't have to tell you how important it is for us to beat Brewster." He paused. "*Everyone* is counting on us," he added, and we knew he was right.

"We'll have two meets against Brewster," he said. Then he stopped talking and gazed up at the sky for what seemed like hours. I let myself sneak a look and saw nothing but blue. "We must break the Brewster curse," he finally said. He studied each of us slowly. "You understand that, boys?"

"Yes, sir!" we all shouted.

Coach nodded. "Fine," he said brusquely.

Then he blew his whistle.

"Move it! Move it!" he shrieked.

We all dove into the pool and did our laps. I felt extra energized. We were going to swim against Brewster!

When I climbed out at the end of practice, I bumped right into Kelly Phillips. She was standing at the pool's edge, and I realized as I crashed into her that she had been watching me in the water. She let out a soft yelp of pain and looked at me with hurt in her beautiful blue eyes.

I was horrified. "I'm sorry," I said miserably. "Are you O.K.?"

She rubbed her arm slowly back and forth. "Just a little bruise," she said softly.

"I'm sorry," I said again. "I didn't see you there."

A twinkle suddenly appeared in her eyes. "Maybe you could make it better," she suggested.

"Sure," I said dumbly.

Kelly waited, a smile on her beautiful face. I watched her, not sure what she wanted me to do. Several minutes passed as we faced each other silently.

"Well?" she asked, holding out her arm to me.

I studied the outstretched arm, knowing it was the most beautiful arm in all of Frog Hollow. She must have sensed my confusion, because she said, "Kiss it to make it better," and indicated the spot where I'd bumped into her.

Kiss Kelly Phillips! My knees unexpectedly buckled, and I almost collapsed backward into the pool. I regained my balance and tried to smile. She smiled back. Trying as best as I could to keep from fainting, I bent down and kissed her arm, unable to believe her beautiful skin was making contact with my mouth. When I straightened up, I had a smile on my face the size of Texas.

For several seconds, we again stood silently. You kissed her! You kissed her! You kissed her! my mind screamed with joy.

"Aren't you going to ask me out?" Kelly said, some impatience creeping into her voice.

How stupid could I be? I opened my mouth, but my voice refused to work. I cleared my throat several times, wishing I wasn't such a geek. Finally I managed to squeak, "Will you go out with me?"

"Yes!" Kelly exclaimed.

I couldn't believe it. Just like that, Kelly Phillips was my girlfriend. She leaned forward and, in one sudden movement, kissed me loudly on the mouth. My heart nearly popped out of my chest.

"I have to go over to my friend's house now, but I'll see you tomorrow," she said.

"O.K.," I croaked.

She waved. I lifted my hand limply. She turned to go, and I stood motionless, my hand still lifted.

I was still standing there when Nick and Garus walked over.

"Hemingway, my man," Nick said. "Way to go!" He slapped me hard on the back.

Garus was grinning madly. "Good show, old bean," he said. "Jolly good show. You are quite talented with the ladies, old boy."

Nick's smile was so big it took up most of his face. "Hemingway," he said again, "I didn't know you had it in you."

"Me neither," I mumbled, following behind them in a kind of mental fog as we walked to the snack bar. My mind was completely filled up with Kelly Phillips. She had kissed me! On the mouth! She was my girlfriend!

"I say, old chaps, there is always a queue at this shop," Garus said indignantly.

Nick turned to him in disgust. "The problem with you, Garus," he said, "is that you're a total loser."

Garus looked hurt for a moment, but then he said, "And the problem with you, old boy, is that you are too big for your britches."

I marveled at Garus. He never talked back to Nick.

Nick, however, was not amused. "Watch it," he said menacingly.

"You don't frighten me, old chap," Garus replied. I couldn't believe it. Garus was on a roll today!

Nick turned and faced Garus. In one quick movement, he had Garus in a headlock.

"Let me go, you bloody ape!" Garus shouted.

"Let him go, Nick," I said wearily.

Nick looked at me. "O.K., Hemingway, but just this once." He let Garus go. Garus rubbed his neck, which had a perfect print of Nick's hand on it.

We finally reached the snack-bar counter. Nick and Garus each ordered a cheeseburger, and I got a soda. When we sat down, Mallory suddenly appeared out of nowhere.

"Hey," she said casually. She was wearing a bathing suit and had a towel wrapped around her waist.

"What are you doing here?" I asked.

Mallory looked at me as if I were a moron. "Swimming," she replied.

"Mallory, babe," Nick drawled, "why don't ya lose that towel so we can check out your fine body?"

Mallory stared at Nick with eyes so fierce I thought he would shrivel up and die. She slowly raised her fist. "Better watch it," she said threateningly, "or you're going to get one of these right in your ugly face."

Nick laughed nervously. "I was just joking with you, baby," he said. "Let's get out of here," he whispered to Garus, and the two of them rose and left.

Mallory watched them go, then turned to me. "How's your novel going, m.p.?" she asked cheerfully. "You getting any good material from here?"

"Oh yeah," I said absently. "It's great. Fantastic. No problem." In my mind I was replaying Kelly Phillips's mouth on mine.

"Good," Mallory said, then fell silent.

"How's your essay?" I asked after a few minutes, in a sudden flash of clarity.

At the mention of her essay, Mallory's eyes clouded over. "Not so good," she said.

"Really?" I asked merrily. A warm feeling washed over me. I wasn't the only person in the world who was having trouble writing. There was someone else—Mallory.

If Mallory heard the delight in my voice, she didn't comment on it. "I don't think it's a winning essay," she explained. Then she added simply, "I'm not a writer." She looked to me for a few words of comfort, but my mind had again taken up with Kelly Phillips. Before I could think of anything to say, Mallory said, "I better get home."

"O.K.," I said happily.

I sat at the snack bar for a long time afterward, consumed with the fact that I had kissed Kelly Phillips. It was only when the snack-bar guy closed up the place that I realized how late it was.

"Hey, kid," he said, "you got a problem or something?"

"No problem," I answered dreamily.

"Good," he replied.

"Good," I repeated, then headed home.

Chapter 8

" *'Kiss me, you fool,' the queen commanded Captain Starpants, but he didn't know which of her three mouths she meant.* **"**

A sci-fi love story between an alien queen and a human space-fleet commander was definitely the way to go. The only problem was, I spent the next hour thinking about Kelly Phillips instead of writing more sentences.

"Being in love isn't so great for writing," I observed out loud, but Mark Twain, Isaac Asimov, and Dashiell Hammett had no comment about that. I did nothing for the next few minutes, and then the telephone rang.

I jumped up, startled out of my lovesickness, and ran into my parents' bedroom to answer it.

"Hemingway! You gotta come over. We need you." Before I could respond, Nick hung up. An obnoxious dial tone rang in my ear.

I stared at the receiver. It occurred to me that Nick did not respect my need for time alone to write. Then again, I wasn't writing much. I decided to go.

I got dressed, choosing whatever clothes were on top of my pile, and headed downstairs. It dawned on me that I probably should clean up my pile and start dressing decently now that I had a girlfriend. My room had to be neater if Kelly ever came over. Kelly Phillips in my room! My heart raced at the thought. I didn't know if I'd be able to survive that.

I had been thinking, now that Kelly and I were going out, that we should be doing, you know, couple stuff. Taking her to the movies was out of the question, since someone would have to drive us, and there was no way I'd let either her father or my parents do that. Taking her out to eat wasn't so easy either, since I didn't have enough money and didn't want to ask Mom or Dad for more. Coming over to my house was the only thing I could think of, even if it was totally lame.

When I got to Nick's, Mrs. Positano directed me through the house and to the backyard, where Nick and Garus were standing around, each holding a toolbox. Next to them was the oldest car I'd ever seen in my life. Nick's older brother, Tommy, was bent over one of the tires, studying it with great concentration.

"Hey, Tommy," Nick called as I approached the dilapidated wreck. "I got 'em, just like I said I would." He smiled and winked at me, and as soon as he did that, I knew we were going to be doing something stupid. I involuntarily let out a groan and surveyed the fenced-in yard, trying to plan a quick escape, but I was stuck.

Tommy eyed us and scowled. He was a huge guy who could tackle the three of us together with one hand *and* one leg tied behind his back.

"All right, losers, listen up!" he bellowed as he straightened up to his full height. I felt like a midget standing next to him. He extended his arm toward the wreck in a movement that mimicked the women on game shows who pointed to prizes, except that no one in their right mind would want to take *this* home with them.

"I bought this for fifty dollars," he said, as if that explained everything. A slow smile formed on his face. "A beauty, ain't she?"

We looked at each other wordlessly. Nick smiled faintly.

"I say, old chap, does the vehicle run?" asked Garus, putting down his toolbox.

Tommy's brow furrowed in anger. "Of course it runs!" he roared. He took a menacing step toward Garus, then thought better of it and returned to his place by the car.

"This baby just needs some old-fashioned TLC, that's all," he said, more to the wreck than to us, "starting with a paint job. You're going to paint my car and do a good job, or *else*," he snarled.

He carefully lined up five pails of paint and a handful of paintbrushes in front of us and proceeded to detail exactly how he wanted the car painted. Nick nodded after every word and even said, "Right on," a couple of times.

Tommy ignored him. He placed a hand lovingly on the car's hood and faced us angrily. "You girls better not mess this up or you'll be asking for it. Pow!" He punched his fist into his hand as if to demonstrate what would happen if we failed him.

At that moment, a bright red convertible screeched to a halt in front of the house. Music blasted out of the car stereo. Two girls, both wearing dark sunglasses and bikini tops, sat in the front seats.

Tommy turned to the convertible and waved. The girls waved back, and one of them lowered her sunglasses and winked. Tommy smiled and blew a kiss to her, then turned back to us.

"My ride's here," he said matter-of-factly. With that, he disappeared into the house. A moment later he got into the convertible and they sped away.

We stood there speechless for several minutes staring after them.

"Why would someone buy a junk car for fifty dollars when he could get a ride like that?" I mumbled.

Nick shook his head. "I don't know, Hemingway," he said sadly. "Wish I had a ride like that. Or even a car." He turned away from us, put down the toolbox he was holding, and busied himself combing his hair. I suddenly realized why Nick thought he had to act so cool. Tommy was a hard act to follow. Maybe having no brothers and sisters wasn't such a bad thing.

Only Garus seemed unaffected. "Shall we get to work, old boys?" he asked brightly.

We both stared at him. "If we don't paint the bloke's car, we'll get ourselves in quite a bit of bloody trouble, I should say," he pointed out.

"Yeah, I guess so," Nick said. He opened the cans of paint and handed us each a paintbrush.

"All right, listen up," he said. "This is how we're going to do it. Hemingway," he barked, "you write '*Playboy* lives' in red."

I saluted Nick, which only encouraged him further.

"Garus," he ordered, "you're doing 'Pop Tarts' in blue."

"Blimey," Garus muttered.

Nick rubbed his hands together. "I'm going to paint our names on the hood."

Garus and I looked up sharply. "I say, old boy," Garus said with concern. "Tommy didn't mention anything about our names on the bonnet—just his name." He added, "Pow, remember?"

Nick waved Garus's concern away. "He just wants it to look cool. Trust me."

"I don't know . . . ," Garus began.

"Trust me," Nick said again. "I know my brother." As if to prove his point, he began painting "JACKIE" in bright yellow paint on the hood.

"Are you deranged? Don't do that!" I yelled. "He'll bash my head in."

"Relax, Hemingway, I know what I'm doing."

Garus and I watched helplessly as Nick painted his name next, then Garus's. I vowed to paint over my name when Nick wasn't looking. I studied the yard again, trying to figure out the quickest way out. Surely there had to be a hole *somewhere* in the fence.

Garus and I reluctantly dipped our brushes in the cans and began working. The air became thick with the smell of paint and sweat. When we were done, we stood back to admire our efforts.

At that moment, Garus slipped on a rock and fell. His paintbrush flew up into the air and landed right on top of Nick's head. A big glob of blue paint slid down his forehead, leaving behind a streak of perfectly combed blue hair.

Nick screamed and put both hands on his head. "You moron!" he shouted at Garus.

Garus got to his feet and cried, "It was an accident," but Nick reached for his paintbrush and flung it at him. Garus ducked, and the brush hit Tommy's car instead. It landed on the roof, skidded across, and slid down the side, leaving a bright orange trail behind it.

Nick threw another paintbrush at Garus and missed again. The brush left another streak across Tommy's car.

"Stop it! Stop it!" I cried, moving in front of Garus. "He'll strangle us! He'll kill us!"

"Out of my way, Hemingway!" Nick shouted as he threw a brush at me. It smacked me right in the nose. Somebody yelled, "Paint fight!" and for the next few minutes a rainbow of paints flew back and forth across the yard.

When it was all over Tommy's car looked like it had been attacked by a squadron of evil paint aliens.

"This sucks," Nick pronounced.

We tried to fix it as best as we could, but we had practically run out of paint. We were almost done when the red convertible again screeched to a halt in front of the house. Tommy got out without turning back to the two girls. He walked into the house and came out to the backyard as the convertible sped away. When he saw his car, his jaw dropped.

"You idiots!" he screamed, ripping off his sunglasses. "What did you do to my car?!"

He turned to us, saliva foaming at the corners of his mouth.

"You stupid, lousy, good-for-nothing, brain-challenged retards!" he shrieked. Turning a shade of tomato red, he took a menacing step toward us.

Whimpering, we each took one step back.

He took two steps forward and raised his fists, growling like a bear.

"Run for it!" Nick shouted, and we all bolted from the yard, through the house, and out to the street with Tommy chasing us, hollering like a lunatic.

At the end of the block we split up and each went in a different direction. Tommy, confused for a moment, decided to chase me.

"Oh my God," I uttered as I glanced over my shoulder at his explosive face. I raced past the community center, past the school, and right past my house without realizing it. Meanwhile, Tommy was getting closer.

Then I remembered that Mr. Conrad's house was on the next block. I turned the corner and headed that way, not daring to look back.

I jumped over Mr. Conrad's picket-fence gate, catching my sneaker on it and tumbling to the ground in front of the house. Tommy was right on my heels. Before I could get up, Mr. Conrad opened the door and peeked out.

I lay there helplessly and covered my head with my hands, waiting for Tommy to pound me into oblivion.

"What's going on?" Mr. Conrad asked when he saw me sprawled on the ground.

Before I could answer, Fifi, who had been standing behind him, raced out just as Tommy jumped over the gate. She barked three times. Tommy let out a frightened howl, scrambled back over the gate, and ran from the house.

Fifi came up to me and licked my face as if nothing had happened. I gaped at her with wonder. Tommy seemed to have the same dog-fearing gene Nick had. A poodle had just saved my life!

Mr. Conrad smiled amiably. "In a bit of trouble there, Jackie?"

"Yes, sir," I answered sheepishly.

"Well, I'm glad Fifi and I could be of service," he said and chuckled to himself.

Fifi barked twice, as if to agree.

Chapter 9

“The first time I saw her, I realized there are times when I really hate that I never forget a face.”

Back to film noir. It was the best choice.

My stomach growled loudly as I hunched over the type-writer. I ignored it and tried to think of a second sentence. It growled again—this time louder. I ignored it again. When it growled for the third time, it sounded like an earthquake had hit Frog Hollow. Even Mark, Isaac, and Dashiell looked worried.

“O.K., O.K.,” I said irritably. “I hear you.” Then I mumbled, “Even my own body is conspiring against my novel.”

Reluctantly, I shut off the typewriter and headed to the kitchen. I fixed myself a salami sandwich from my own private stash of food. Lately I’d been keeping salami and jellybeans hidden behind the three gallons of soy milk in the fridge. If Mom ever discovered them, she’d probably throw a fit, accusing me of contaminating her "healthful kitchen." I wrapped the sandwich discreetly in aluminum foil and headed back to my room.

"Jackie!" Mom called up just then. "We're going to the Health and Nutrition Show over in Matawan. Want to come along?"

Mom needed an answer to that question?

"No thanks!" I yelled down. Why she thought I'd want to spend the day consorting with weirdos and freaks from all over the state is beyond me.

There was a knock on my door. "Jackie, it's me," Mom said, opening the door and coming inside. "Why don't you come along with us?"

"No thanks," I said, watching her eye my sandwich with displeasure. She frowned, but made no comment about it.

"Who knows—it might inspire you," she said, gesturing to my typewriter.

I looked at her like she'd just landed from Mars. How a Health and Nutrition Show could be inspiring was also beyond me.

"I have to be at the swim club today," I said, which was partly true. There was no practice, but I'd told Nick and Garus I'd meet them there later.

"All right," she said. She started to leave, then turned around. "By the way," she said, "I know all about your salami and jellybeans. You don't have to hide these things from us."

I said nothing in response. I was too busy wondering how she found them. Only Dad handled the soy milk, and with his coffee weakness, I thought he'd probably understand about salami and jellybeans.

"You might as well know," Mom said, using her editor voice, "salami is one of the worst foods you can eat."

I picked up my sandwich and defiantly chomped down on it. Mom shook her head and left the room.

"Salami may be one of the worst foods you can eat, but at least it tastes good," I said to no one in particular. I finished my sandwich and licked my fingers. The only thing that concerned me about salami was the possibility that I might have salami breath, which can be pretty lethal. Believe me, I know. Nick's family has salami every other week, and on the days they do you can't walk into their house without a gas mask.

I decided to gargle with Dad's organically grown spearmint mouthwash. "Fresh Breath the Natural Way," the bottle read. I poured a cupful and swished it around my mouth, feeling it suddenly burn my flesh. I spit it out, my mouth completely singed. I studied the bottle again. What was in this stuff—gasoline? Well, at least there was no trace of salami on my breath.

I went back to my room and decided to choose clothing from my pile with care—for a change. I settled on a pair of khaki shorts and a blue T-shirt. Then I headed out.

When I got to the swim club, I found Nick and Garus in the locker room. Nick was in front of a mirror frantically combing his hair. He had a panic-stricken look on his face. Garus stood nearby, watching Nick with worry.

"Hey, guys," I said. "What's going on?"

Nick whipped around to face me. "Thank God you're here, Hemingway," he said. He grabbed me by the shoulders. "How do I look?" He stepped back and turned his head to the side.

I snorted. "What's going on?" I asked again.

"Just tell me how I look," Nick pleaded.

"You look like you always do," I said contemptuously. Then for the third time I asked, "What's going on?"

Nick ignored me, turned back to the mirror, and pulled the comb through his hair savagely. Garus looked at me. "Your lady has informed us that one of her associates fancies his company," he said, hitching his thumb at Nick.

I glared at Garus, then at Nick. "Can you repeat that in English? American English?" I said scornfully.

Garus gave a loud sigh, then opened his mouth again, but before he could get anything out, Nick looked at me and cried, "It's a chick, Hemingway!" Then he mumbled, "I gotta get my hair right," and turned back to the mirror.

Garus cleared his throat importantly. "One of Kelly Phillips's associates—" he began.

"One of her friends likes me," Nick interrupted, and he sounded like he couldn't believe it either.

"Really?" I asked incredulously.

Garus nodded grimly.

"Which one?" I asked, even though it wouldn't have mattered if they'd told me, since I didn't know any of her friends' names.

"We have not yet been informed as to that particular matter," Garus replied stiffly. He let out another sigh, as if the weight of being Nick's friend was becoming too heavy a load for him to bear. "Perhaps you had better carry on out there while we get some bloody things in order here," he suggested, and I managed to understand that he meant for me to go back outside.

"O.K.," I replied, only too happy to leave the bizarre scene. As I walked out to the pool, I turned in the direction of the snack bar and suddenly felt two hands from behind cover my eyes.

"Guess who?" she asked, and the feel of her so close made me dizzy.

She lifted her hands and turned me around. She smiled, and I smiled back, unable to take my eyes off her yellow bikini. She leaned forward and kissed me on the mouth. "Hi," she said.

"Hi," I muttered, bowled over by the kiss.

She took my hand and pulled me forward. "Charlene likes your friend," she confided. "Maybe we could double-date." She exploded into the most adorable giggles in the world.

"O.K.," I said stupidly.

At that moment, a group of girls approached us from the snack bar. They were all in bikinis and were all chewing gum, and it occurred to me that they all looked pretty much alike. One of them blew a big pink bubble that collapsed onto her face. I wondered if she was Charlene.

"Hi, Kelly," they said together.

Before Kelly could respond, the sound of barking dogs made us all turn around. Another girl in a bikini was standing just outside the swim-club gates, petting three German shepherds. The dogs were jumping up and licking her face and she was laughing.

"Charlene! We're over here!" Kelly called, and the girl looked up at the mention of her name.

As soon as I connected the girl to the dogs I knew this could only mean trouble.

At that moment Nick, with Garus following close behind, came out of the locker room. He had a huge smile plastered on his face. His hair was slicked back as if it were held with glue. He approached us using his macho-stride walk.

Once he reached us he asked smoothly, "Which one of you beautiful girls is Charlene?" I couldn't help but be impressed. When Nick pulled himself together, he really performed. Must come from watching Tommy so much, I thought.

The girls all smiled shyly, and I could tell each one of them wanted to be Charlene at that particular moment. They looked toward the gates, and Nick followed their gaze, just in time to see Charlene passionately kissing the three dogs. She looked up and waved.

The smile on Nick's face quickly faded away. "Oh my God," he said to himself. "It can't be."

Charlene left the dogs and came through the gates. She walked toward us and stopped in front of Nick. "Hi," she said breathlessly.

Perhaps it was because she was so beautiful. More likely it was the obvious fact that Charlene loved dogs. Whatever it was, Nick's eyes rolled back into his head, and he crumpled in a heap to the ground.

One of the girls screamed. Garus gasped. Charlene watched helplessly. Kelly ran to the lifeguard station. A burly lifeguard whom everyone called Stinky raced over.

"Give him some air!" he instructed roughly, and I suddenly felt like we were being filmed for a TV medical show.

At last, after several minutes, Nick came to. He sat up, bewildered, and slowly gazed at the faces of the people who had gathered around him in a circle.

"Are you O.K.?" Charlene asked.

Nick looked at Charlene's beautiful face, but the fear in his eyes spelled "German shepherd."

"I don't feel so good," he said weakly.

"All right, everybody, scram!" Stinky commanded. He helped Nick up, walked him over to the lifeguard station, and called his parents. Tommy was dispatched to come and pick him up—in the wreck, now repainted a smoky green. It belched and coughed up to the front of the swim club, where Nick was waiting with Stinky. Tommy didn't even look at Nick when he got into the car but kept his eyes straight ahead, no doubt ashamed of his brother's behavior. They drove away, leaving the stench of burnt oil behind them.

The crowd watched them leave, then collectively shook their heads and returned to sunbathing and swimming. Kelly turned to Charlene and said, "I'm so sorry, Charlene." Then she asked Garus and me, "What happened?"

"Heatstroke, my dear," Garus answered crisply. "Terrible case of heatstroke."

Kelly and Charlene nodded solemnly, and I could see that they felt sorry for Nick. I could also tell that this episode of "heatstroke" would only increase Charlene's ardor.

I exchanged glances with Garus. He was brilliant, and a true friend to the very end.

Chapter 10

> "Tyra the Fair slowly approached the castle. The knights in black armor who guarded the gates unsheathed their long swords and pointed them at her. 'I come in peace,' she said, and slowly they lowered their swords and, finally, sheathed them."

Fantasy, not film noir, is the way to go. You know, fire-breathing dragons, jousting knights, castles, wizards.

I was secretly thrilled that I had managed to write three sentences instead of one this time, but I still needed a lot more, and though I sat at the typewriter for hours, nothing happened. And then it was time for swim practice.

I pulled on my bathing suit, my heart racing at the idea of seeing Kelly again. I hadn't even gotten to first base with her yet. First base was French kissing, according to Nick. I didn't know what French kissing was, but I wasn't about to tell him that. Besides, Nick had his own problems. After his fainting episode, he asked Garus to give him "dog lessons," that is, instructions on how to act around dogs. Nick was determined to go out with Charlene. Not only was she beautiful, but she liked him. You couldn't ask for more than that, and Nick wasn't about to let a lifelong fear of dogs or her three German shepherds get in his way.

When I got to the swim club, I noticed a lot more people there than usual, and then it hit me. The Brewster team was there! Coach had mentioned this at the last practice, but I had been too busy thinking about his daughter to remember what he said. It was something about the Brewster team needing to use our pool because theirs was being fixed. Of all the swim clubs in the area, why did they have to choose ours? We were the next town over, that's true, but couldn't they have gone to Marlboro?

I caught sight of Nick and Garus by the snack bar. "Hey, guys," I said, walking over.

Nick grunted, then took his comb out. "You see those Brewster guys? They just try something, they're asking for it." He said this so convincingly that I almost believed him.

Garus eyed him, then said, "You've obviously not paid attention to the lessons of history. Don't you remember the colonies—the empire? Violence, old chaps, is never the answer."

"Yeah, but what's the question?" Nick said, then guffawed at his own stupid joke. Ever since Charlene had shown an interest in him—dogs notwithstanding—Nick thought he was cooler than ever.

Mallory was swimming in the pool. She climbed out, reached for a towel, and walked over to us. "Hi, guys," she said. She indicated the Brewster team, which was doing laps on the left side of the pool. "Bet you're q.i.y.b." (Quaking in your boots.)

"Quite so," Garus said, nodding his head. For some reason, he seemed to have an enormous aptitude for understanding Mallory. Besides me, he was the only one who knew her abbreviations. Maybe it was because he spoke a different language, too.

Nick scowled. "Bring 'em on," he said. "I can take 'em."

Mallory smiled, more out of pity than amusement. She studied the other team for a moment. "They sure are big," she said, and she was right. The Brewster swimmers were *massive*.

"Brains, baby," Nick drawled. "That's what matters."

"Well, you're in bigger trouble than I thought," she replied.

Garus snorted as Nick scowled again. "It's too bad I'm accounted for, Mallory, babe," he said nonchalantly. "Otherwise you may have had a chance."

Mallory raised her eyebrows. "P.m.," she said cheerfully. (Poor me.) "You didn't have to drug her, did you?"

"Ha ha ha," Nick replied. "For your information—"

Just then Coach blew his whistle, calling us to practice. We left Mallory, trotted to the pool's edge, and lined up.

"Boys," Coach said somberly, "the moment of truth is upon us." He pulled a pear out of his pocket and took a ferocious bite out of it. For a few minutes, he silently watched us and chomped on his pear.

"We don't need any trouble," he finally said. "You hear me, boys?"

"Yes, sir!"

"I'm counting on you to swim, not get into trouble," he said.

"Yes, sir!"

He looked at each of us in turn. When he got to me, he took a gigantic bite out of his pear, staring into my eyes and chewing at the same time. "You hear me?" he asked again, and I felt as if he was directing the question right at me.

"Yes, sir!"

Without actually saying so, Coach was obviously referring to the Brewster team, and I could imagine exactly the kind of trouble he meant. He held what was left of the pear at arm's length in front of him. A small kid came out of nowhere and took it away.

Free of the pear, Coach clapped his hands twice. "Boys, you're going to be swimming side by side with *them*." He said "them" as if they had horrible contagious diseases. "Just . . . swim. You got it?"

"Yes, sir!"

"All right, White, you're up."

Garus dived in and began his laps. One could never tell whether Coach would start from the beginning of the alphabet or the end of the alphabet when he called us. Sometimes he'd call out names at random. He did it "t.k.u.o.o.t.," Mallory said. (To keep us on our toes.)

The Brewster team was truly swimming side by side with us, and I was in the lane closest to them. I peeked over and saw six feet of blubber standing next to me. "Heard you're the best swimmer on the team," the blubber growled.

Stunned, I gaped at him. No one had ever told me I was the best swimmer on the team, though I probably was. The last thing I needed, though, was to confirm that to this goon. I didn't say anything in response.

"You got a tongue?" he snarled.

I shrugged.

"Watch it," he said, "or I'll pull your tongue right out of your ugly mouth."

"Oh, shut up," I said without thinking.

The blubber looked at me with disbelief. "You're in big trouble now," he said ominously, moving closer. I put out my hand to stop him, inadvertently giving him a slight shove. The blubber lost his balance and fell clumsily into the water. I looked at his flailing form with horror.

What had I done?!

The shrieking of Coach's whistle interrupted my growing panic. "Monterey!" he was yelling. "Get over here NOW!"

I made my way to Coach, sneaking a glance at the goon climbing out of the pool. He was glaring at me with pure venom in his eyes.

"Monterey," Coach said through clenched teeth, "I thought I told you to swim and not make trouble."

"I didn't mean to—"

"I thought I made that clear."

"But I really didn't—"

"I don't want to hear your sorry excuses." Coach leaned forward until our noses almost touched. "Do you want to get kicked off this team?"

I hesitated, considering it. "No," I finally said.

Coach straightened up. He studied me for a full minute. I wondered what he was thinking and whether it had anything to do with Kelly. Is that why he was always so hard on me? I

71

wondered. I started to feel uncomfortable under his gaze but continued to look back at him.

"Monterey, I'm going to let you do your laps," Coach said at last. He studied my reaction, which was a blank stare. "This is your last chance," he said gruffly. "You got that?"

I nodded.

He motioned for me to get in the water. I walked to the pool's edge, dove in, and did my laps, keeping an eye out for the goon. When I climbed out of the water, Nick and Garus were at the snack bar, and the goons were nowhere to be found.

"I saw what you did, Hemingway," Nick said to me. "Nice work, man."

I winced. "I didn't *mean* to do that," I said morosely. I peered discreetly around the snack bar. "Now he's going to kill me!"

Nick looked at me like I was crazy. "Brains, Hemingway. That's all we need to take care of him."

I didn't know what Nick was getting at with his constant talk of "brains"—of which he had none. And I didn't care either. I was a dead man. "Who is he?" I asked.

"Cyrus the Virus Livingston," Garus replied succinctly.

"Cyrus the Virus?"

"Yeah, they call him that because when he's done with you, you feel real sick," Nick said.

Great. That was just what I needed. To get beaten up by a bully with a virus nickname. I was about to say something to that effect when Garus spotted some of the goons. Frantically I turned to look at them, but Cyrus the Virus wasn't among them. A short person was capturing their undivided attention. It was a girl. I leaned forward, trying to make her out. I hoped it wasn't Kelly, or even Charlene. Nick was squinting into the sun, hoping the same thing, I'm sure.

All of a sudden, one of the goons moved away from the others, and the girl went with him. Nick, Garus, and I all gasped in unison. The girl was none other than Mallory, and she was heading right toward the snack bar.

"Consorting with the enemy," Garus said, as if reading my mind.

They waited in line as we watched them with our mouths wide open. The goon bought Mallory a soda and got himself a candy bar. Then Mallory led him right to our table. "Boys," she said, "this is Edgar."

I didn't know what to do first. Laugh at the goon's name. Ask Mallory what she thought she was doing. Tell her about Cyrus the Virus's price on my head.

"Edgar recites poetry," she said with a sparkle in her eyes, and I felt insanely jealous all of a sudden.

Chapter 11

“ ‘Kill him,’ Madame le Edgarova instructed
the gang. ‘If he can’t recite
poetry with the rest of us, he’s history.’ ”

It was getting embarrassingly late in the summer and I still
hadn’t gotten past the opening lines of my novel. I really
had to get moving. The good part was that Kelly was away
for two weeks, visiting her mother, so I had more time to
write. That is, if you didn’t count the infinite distractions
Nick and Garus threw at me.

The phone rang. I didn’t answer, determined to ignore
them and continue writing. When the answering machine
picked up, whoever it was hung up. A minute later the phone
rang again. Again I let it ring, and again they hung up.
When it rang for the fifth time, I figured I should probably
answer it. Maybe it wasn’t them—maybe it was an emergency.

Maybe it was my parents calling from their weirdo convention in Jamesburg.

"Hemingway!"

"Nick?"

"Hallo, old boy."

"Garus?"

For the next few minutes they tried to convince me to join them on their latest stupid adventure.

"We're checking out a sewer pipe Garus found," Nick informed me matter-of-factly. "It's gonna be great, Hemingway."

I paused. "You're checking out a sewer pipe and it's going to be great?" Somehow, those two things didn't make sense to me.

"That's what I said the first time."

"Well, have fun."

"Hey, you gotta come."

"Sorry, I can't."

"Why not?"

"'Cause I'm busy."

"Busy doing what?"

"Writing."

A pause. "Whatcha writing about?" It was the first time Nick had ever asked that question. It disarmed me so much that I found myself describing my gangster epic to him. I made the mistake of mentioning my other attempts, too.

"Hey, you know what, Hemingway?" Nick said. "That sci-fi one with the aliens? You should inject some technology-gone-wrong into that."

"Technology-gone-wrong?" I repeated suspiciously. I

hated to admit it, but the suggestion kind of intrigued me. "You think so?" I asked.

"Definitely," Nick continued. "Let's see. How about this. The polar ice caps melt. The earth is flooded. The aliens want the water."

"Exploring the sewer pipe might trigger some flood ideas for you, old bean," Garus added.

"Yeah, that's what I was gonna say," Nick said with irritation.

I considered it. "You really think it would help?" I asked like a moron.

"Absolutely, Hemingway."

Hmmm. *Waterworld* meets *Alien*. It was a great idea. And I could definitely see the movie possibilities. I could imagine the headlines: Young Writer Signs Twenty Million Dollar Film Deal. Monterey Selects A-List Actor for Role of WaterMan. Teen Novelist's Sci-fi Flood Epic a Worldwide Sensation.

"All right, guys, I'll be over in a minute," I said excitedly. I went to my room and pulled on old scuffed boots and my most beat-up jeans. Then I went to Nick's house, where the sewer expedition was to depart.

After walking along the creek behind Nick's house for some time we reached the sewer opening. The concrete pipe was just high enough so that if you stood straight up, your cranium grazed the ceiling. I couldn't believe we were actually inside our drainage system. Garus had discovered the pipe a few days before, and it immediately became the town's newest playground, although I hadn't been in it and had missed the significant day when Tommy rode his mountain bike through it from one end to the other.

The tea-brown water was pretty deep to start off with, reaching up to our knees. I stared into the blackness ahead of me and could vaguely make out an outline of Garus, who was taking to the water like an alligator. Then the water began to recede and only came up to our ankles. I could tell as soon as I entered the pipe that it would not help me write a sci-fi flood novel. But it was too late. I glared angrily at the back of Nick's head. "Stupid *Waterworld*," I muttered.

Soon the light from behind us died out, and we were walking in total darkness, punctuated by much cursing. Garus switched on his flashlight and was promptly greeted with cries of "Shut that stupid thing off!"

Suddenly, there was a huge noise. "Cops!" shouted Nick.

"Quiet, man!" Garus yelled. It was his flashlight, which had smashed to bits against the wall when he slipped.

We continued grimly on our march. In the distance—a light. We surged forward with renewed vigor. Alas, it was just a sewer grating.

We looked up and saw two spectators peering down at us. They were the two girls from the red convertible. We greeted them with cries of:

"Come on down, babe!"

"Maybe we could do some water aerobics!"

"We'll come up and get ya!"

The girls responded by throwing clumps of dirt at us.

"Let's get out of here!" Nick screamed.

We left them behind and continued into the blackness. We were in the darkest part of the tunnel now. I could not make out a single thing in front of me. I groped blindly at the walls and hoped there were no dangerous creatures lurking at these depths, such as man-eating eels and the like.

Suddenly, there was another light in the distance! Nick and I broke into a run and soon reached the end of the pipe. At last, we emerged out of darkness and into the sunlight. I turned my attention to Nick, who I was determined to strangle, but before I could do so, Garus popped out of the tunnel.

"We did it, old boys," he cried, holding his arms up like a boxer.

I glared at him. He would be next on my strangulation list.

No sooner had he come out than Garus turned around and went right back in. Nick followed. Cursing, I paced the opening for a while before doing the same. How else was I going to get home?

On the return trip we moved at a faster pace. Garus passed under the grating first, only to be spit upon by the two girls. In retaliation, he threw handfuls of water up at them.

Nick prepared to move under the grating quickly, lest he be covered with spit, too. He jumped across and landed with a splash on the other side. I did the same but slipped when I landed. Although I was able to save myself, I had splashed Nick from head to toe.

"Hemingway, you dirty—"

I quickly squirmed past him and ran ahead before he could drench me. Finally, I reached the end. When I emerged from the pipe, I got a huge splash of water in my face. Garus cracked up.

I looked at him in disbelief. "I am going to kill you," I said calmly.

Just then Nick emerged. I turned to him. "I am going to kill you, too," I said.

"Jackie, my man," Nick replied nonchalantly, taking out his comb. "That was fun, wasn't it?"

"No, it was not," I said, starting to walk away.

"Hey," Nick called. "Where you going?"

I ignored him and kept going.

"Hey, come back. We're not done."

I turned around. "I'm done. I, John Monterey Jr., am done!" I yelled crazily. What made them think I'd enjoy this stupidity? I had serious work to do. Nobody took my writing seriously but me. I was going home to my novel and that was that.

But the only idea I could come up with once I sat myself in front of my typewriter was Tyra the Fair teaming up with Faka Kulu in the year 2063 to battle a race of mutant owls for domination of the universe. For the first time that summer, I flung my *GET RICH QUICK!* writing book across the room.

Chapter 12

"On March 24, 2074, the polar ice caps melted, flooding the earth and forcing men to sprout fins."

With Kelly gone and Nick and Garus now banished from my life forever, I thought I'd do some real writing. Except for swim practice, I didn't move from my typewriter, and I ignored Nick and Garus when I saw them at the swim club. But I was still getting stuck on my opening line, and there seemed to be nothing I could do about it. Still, I vowed not to give up. I was going to write *something* this summer.

After four days of secluding myself in my room, however, I started getting cabin fever. So I decided to hear out Nick and Garus when they showed up on my doorstep to grovel for my friendship.

"Hemingway, we're real sorry," Nick said, trying to look contrite.

"Profoundly so, old boy," Garus added solemnly.

"We're real, real sorry," Nick said again.

"Extremely so," Garus chimed in.

"We're so sorry that . . ." Nick glanced at Garus for help. Garus seemed equally stumped.

"That . . ." Nick tried again.

"I dunno," Garus finally whispered to Nick.

They gazed at me helplessly. "We're real sorry," Nick said.

"All right, all right," I said. "You're real sorry. Fine."

Nick's face brightened. "So we're friends again?" He didn't wait for me to respond. "Want to come over tomorrow night? My parents are going to be out."

The funny part was, after four days of solitary confinement in my room, I did want to come over. But I didn't want to do anything stupid. Nick seemed to sense this. "We could practice our laps," he suggested earnestly.

It was true that Nick had a swimming pool, but I needed extra insurance. I needed a guarantee that swimming wouldn't degenerate into stupidity.

"Let's get Mallory to pretend to be Coach," I suggested. I figured with Mallory there, things would remain normal.

"O.K.," Nick readily agreed. He took his comb out and ran it through his hair as if in anticipation of having a girl over. "Don't you worry, Hemingway. I'll ask her myself." He grinned, relishing the thought of it.

"Oh no you don't," I said. "I will do the asking, thank you very much." I didn't trust Nick for a minute.

He shrugged and jammed his comb back into his pocket. It occurred to me that he should have a special holster made for it so he could have easier access.

"Well, see you tomorrow," he said, holding out his hand.

I looked at his extended hand, too suspicious to take it. But I didn't want to hurt Nick's feelings, so I put out my hand and we shook without incident. "Later, man," he said, and he and Garus left.

I decided to make my request to Mallory in person, so I got dressed and headed over there. When I arrived at her house, I saw to my horror that Edgar the goon was just leaving. I hid behind a telephone pole as he lumbered off.

"Traitor," I said through gritted teeth as I walked to the front door. I felt peculiar feelings—jealousy, revulsion, rage—all at the same time. I rang the doorbell, and Mallory came to the door.

"Hi, m.p.," she said cheerily.

"Hi," I replied, then fell silent, not knowing what to say. "How are you?" I finally managed.

"Excellent," she said, and I suddenly noticed she was flushed. "Come on in." She opened the door and led me into the kitchen. We sat down at the table.

"Want some snickerdoodles?" she asked, passing me a plate piled high with cinnamon-dusted cookies. "Edgar and I just made them."

The phrase "Edgar and I" made me want to barf just then, making it highly unlikely that I could eat a cookie. "Uh, no thanks," I said hoarsely. I cleared my throat noisily.

"We recited poetry, too," Mallory said, her eyes shining.

I coughed. I looked at the cookies and then at Mallory, trying to imagine her and Edgar reciting poetry.

"'I think that I shall never see,'" Edgar would say.

"'A poem lovely as a tree,'" Mallory would say.

"'A tree whose hungry mouth is prest,
Against the earth's sweet flowing breast;
A tree that looks at God all day,
And lifts her leafy arms to pray,'" Edgar would say. He'd smile stupidly at Mallory, then continue:
"'A tree that may in Summer wear
A nest of robins in her hair;
Upon whose bosom snow has lain;
Who intimately lives with rain.'"
"'Poems are made by fools like me,'" Mallory would say.
"'But only God can make a tree,'" Edgar would say.
"Oh, Edgar!"
"Oh, Mallory!"
I shook my head vigorously, not wanting to ever think about *that* again.

Mallory was watching me closely. "Something wrong, m.p.?"

I gazed at my best friend. It occurred to me that with Mallory working on her essay and me so focused on my novel, I hadn't seen much of her lately. I suddenly felt an overwhelming sadness.

"Edgar is a goon," I said flatly.

Mallory looked at me calmly. "He is not a goon," she said.

"Don't you know about Cyrus the Virus?"

"They're cousins. That doesn't make Edgar a goon."

"Cousins?" I asked.

"That's why they hang out together. Edgar doesn't want to hurt his feelings."

"Cyrus the Virus has feelings?"

Mallory glared at me but didn't respond.

"Well, if you ask me, he's guilty by association," I said right-eously.

"Did you come here for a specific purpose, m.p.?" Mallory said, and I suddenly felt very strange. What if Mom and Dad were right when they said my relationship with Mallory would someday change? A shudder went up and down my spine.

"Are you and Edgar . . . friends?"

Mallory nodded. "Yup," she said.

I snorted. "Boys and girls can't be friends."

Mallory looked at me like I was crazy. "What are *we* then?"

"*Best* friends," I said quickly. "Boys and girls can be *best* friends, but not friends."

"I think you've been spending too much time alone in your room," she replied.

"I'm just letting you know, Mallory, that's all," I said.

"T.y.v.m.," she said, taking a cookie and biting into it. (Thank you very much.) "Is there something I can do for you, m.p.?"

I winced as she chewed the cookie, but her question made me remember why I was there. "Will you pretend to be Coach at Nick's house tomorrow night?"

"Sure," she answered, and I felt like we were back to our old selves. Only Mallory could have understood what I'd just said. I grinned happily.

"You sure you don't want any cookies?" she asked again, pushing the plate toward me.

I flinched, moving away from it. "Oh no," I said. Eating

the cookies she and Edgar made together was like . . . watching them kissing.

Kissing! Oh my God!

"You're not kissing him, are you?" I asked crazily.

Mallory gave me a long look. "Not yet," she said coolly.

"I gotta go," I said abruptly, getting up so quickly my chair almost fell over. I practically ran from the kitchen and out the door. Mallory stood at the door and watched me, a sad expression on her face.

On the way back to my house, I wrestled with feelings I'd never had before, not knowing quite how to react to them. I wished there was someone I could talk to. Then I ran into Nick in front of Mr. Conrad's house. He was holding Fifi on a leash.

"Hey, Hemingway," he said casually. Fifi was engrossed in sniffing the base of a tree. My face must have registered immense confusion, because Nick said, "Mr. Conrad says I can practice the dog skills Garus is teaching me on Fifi." He eyed the dog nervously. "It's not so bad. It's kind of fun."

"My God," I mumbled, "everything's changing. Everyone's losing their minds!"

Nick studied me with concern. "What's the matter, Hemingway?" he asked.

I looked at him with despair in my eyes. "What would you do if your best friend decided to be friends with the cousin of a goon who wanted to beat you up?"

Nick gazed at me blankly. "You feeling all right, Hemingway?"

"I gotta go," I said and ran past him and Fifi.

"Don't forget about tomorrow," he called after me.

Chapter 13

"'I don't think you should give up your job at the chicken coop,' she said after she read my first draft."

A novel about writing a novel? Well, I thought it would work really well, but it was as bad as the others.

"I'm having a rough time here," I said to my fish, but Mark, Isaac, and Dashiell seemed unconcerned. After what happened yesterday, I wasn't in much of a writing mood anyway. I still didn't know what to think of Mallory and Edgar—or Nick and Fifi. But it was almost time to head over to Nick's, and I was hoping that everything would magically be back to normal when I got there.

Nick answered the door when I arrived. He was in his bathing suit, which was a very good sign. Garus was there too, also in a bathing suit. Mallory arrived a short time after

I did, and just as I hoped, began efficiently organizing everyone.

She started by blowing a plastic orange whistle that looked as if it had come out of a cereal box and sounded like the mating call of a mutant coyote.

"Listen up!" she cried as we lined up at the pool, more out of habit than anything else. She walked up and down the line surveying us just as Coach did. She had even brought a banana with her.

"We're going to swim hard tonight," she said, pointing the banana at us. "Real, real hard."

Garus started laughing and then we all cracked up. But Mallory would have none of that. She blew her whistle again and shouted, "Move it! Move it!"

We dove in and did our laps, each of us doing about thirty before Mallory called us out. We rested for a few minutes, then did another thirty. Finally, Mallory made us do ten more before pronouncing that we were done for the night. We lounged on chairs near the pool.

"You need to be ready for your meet against Brewster," Mallory said, and at the mention of Brewster I thought of Edgar the goon. I wondered whose side she was on and was about to ask her when Nick abruptly made an announcement.

"Hemingway," he said with a grin, "you and me are going to entertain two luscious ladies here on Saturday."

"What are you talking about?" I asked irritably. Nick's ladies' man routine was starting to get on my nerves.

Nick grinned wider. "Me, you, Kelly, and *Charlene*." He smacked his lips.

"Huh?" I replied.

"A double date, you dope," Nick said, punching me in the arm. "I've planned a double date for us."

"What?!" I exclaimed, feeling terror grip my body.

Nick nodded solemnly. "That's right," he said. "Your wildest dreams are coming true."

A double date with Nick! This was more like my worst nightmare. With Nick in charge of things, who knew what stupidity would occur—and all in front of Kelly and Charlene!

Mallory smiled at me. "Sounds like some enchanted evening," she said, then cracked up.

Only Garus looked morose. Nick glanced at him triumphantly, but Garus just let out a long sigh. Nick ignored him. Then a peculiar light came into his eyes.

"Hey," he said, "I almost forgot." He got up from his chair and returned holding a small tape recorder. He grinned at us. "Let's curse into this and then replay it."

Mallory rolled her eyes. So, now the stupidity begins, I thought, and with this double date coming up, it will never end. Still, it was pretty early, and we had done a lot of laps. Why not humor Nick and let him go ahead with his stupid idea?

We spent half an hour cursing into the tape recorder. It *was* kind of funny, though Mallory didn't think so. She sat on a lounge chair reading a book of poetry. It made me think of Edgar again. Would everything Mallory did from now on make me think of Edgar?

She saw me staring at her. "I've decided to write a poem about a t.p.," she told me. (Theme park.)

I didn't know what to say, but found myself asking, "Does Edgar like theme parks?"

"Yes," she replied. "Edgar is a person of many interests."

"Good for Edgar," I muttered, not sure if I wanted her to hear me or not. In any case, she did not respond.

Nick, oblivious to our conversation, stood up and announced, "It's chowtime." With Nick, chowtime meant food *and* entertainment. The Positano family not only liked to eat well, they liked to be dramatic about it, and Nick was no exception. He took out his comb to groom for the event.

We followed him inside and seated ourselves at the dining room table. This was a tradition, and it included being served cake, usually chocolate.

"No cake today," Nick said.

"What?" cried Garus.

"We're having apple pie instead."

"Damn it."

I must take a deep breath before I describe the way Nick served the apple pie. First, he ran to the table from the kitchen with four huge slices of pie. Then he returned with a carton of vanilla ice cream and scooped a lopsided lump on each slice. He then charged back into the kitchen and brought out a jar of rainbow sprinkles, which he poured over each ice-cream scoop. With one last gasp he ran back and returned to put one animal cracker on top of each scoop. He then collapsed on the table as we applauded his performance.

"The service here stinks," Mallory observed.

"Hey," Garus whined, "there aren't enough sprinkles on mine!"

Nick scowled, then walked over to Garus's place with the jar of sprinkles in his hand.

"I say, old boy, I'll do it," Garus said nervously.

"No, *I'll* do it," Nick replied mischievously.

Just then, Mallory hit his elbow, tipping an avalanche of sprinkles onto the pie.

"Look what you've done!" Garus cried. He reached for Nick, but Nick dodged him and hid behind my chair.

"Can I please have some soda?" Mallory asked, thankfully interrupting the coming melee.

Nick, in another demonstration of deranged drama, grabbed a liter of Coke and some glasses from the kitchen. He raised the bottle three feet above his head, pouring the dark liquid in a long arc into the waiting glasses.

We cracked up. We couldn't help it. Garus laughed so hard he fell on the floor. Mallory followed. My whole chair tipped over, and I fell backward. At last we returned to our seats and devoured the pie. It didn't take very long.

Afterward, feeling full and sleepy, we stumbled into the living room, and Garus exclaimed, "I say, chaps, let's partake of the naked channel on the telly." He turned on the TV and seated himself on the floor in front of it. Nick ignored him and went into the kitchen to wash the dishes.

"Psst," Mallory whispered to me, "let's push Garus into the shower and turn on the water."

"O.K.," I said, marveling at her cunning.

"You wait in the bathroom, and I'll bring him there," she instructed.

"Very good," I answered, nodding my head.

I disappeared into the bathroom. A minute later Mallory came in with Garus. "It's right there," she said to him.

Garus leaned over the tub, looking for the squirrel Mallory had told him was lounging there. At that moment, I emerged from behind the shower curtain and joined Mallory in pushing Garus into the tub.

"I say, what's going on," he demanded, waving his arms about. In an attempt to save himself, he grabbed onto the shower curtain but fell anyway. So did the curtain—rod and all. I turned on a short burst of water.

As Garus lay flailing in the tub and Mallory and I cracked up, Nick came into the bathroom. When we saw his expression we stopped laughing and silently studied the deformed shower curtain rod.

"It's bent!" he screamed.

"I'll fix it," I offered. I took the rod and pounded it until I succeeded in bending it the other way.

"It will break, man!" shouted Garus, grabbing it from me.

Before Garus could do anything, Nick grabbed it from him, looking like he was about to cry. "They're going to kill me," he whimpered.

"Here, let me," Mallory said, grabbing it from him.

She managed to bend the rod back into shape, and we hung the shower curtain over the bump in the middle of it. But, as we were to find out later, we had put it on backward. Mrs. Positano took away Nick's allowance for two weeks to pay for a new rod.

A few minutes later, for no specific reason, Garus and Mallory decided to dance around the living room singing "The Star-Spangled Banner" at the top of their lungs. Nick stood watching them in disbelief, then angrily pointed his finger at the door. So, naturally, they marched outside—still singing.

I think the night's level of stupidity had exceeded what even Nick could tolerate, especially since it was happening in his house. "Tell those jerks to shut up," he said wearily, regretting that he had ever asked us to come over.

I found the two of them in the backyard. Garus was dancing on the patio table and Mallory was serenading him.

"Are you crazy? Get down from there!" I yelled, wondering what in the world had gotten into them, though it was amusing, I had to admit.

Garus stepped to the side of the table, and it fell over with a deafening crash. For a moment we were all silent.

Garus looked up at me from the ground. I stared back at him.

"Let's get out of here!" Mallory yelled.

We bolted through the house and out the door, not stopping till we were about a mile away from Nick's house. We stood silently, trying to catch our breath.

"Gentlemen," Garus said stiffly, "I salute you." And he turned to head home. Mallory and I glanced at each other, then did the same.

Chapter 14

> "After the terrifying new bomb was unleashed, the sun did not rise again. A cold, dark world took over the planet Earth—a world where only nocturnal ones survived."

A gloomy post-apocalyptic thriller was about the way I was feeling right now. The double date that Nick had planned was making me so nervous I thought I might have a stroke and never even get there. My stomach was a jumble of nerves and butterflies, and my hands shook as I stood in front of my mirror trying to do something about my hair.

For the most part, I looked all right. I was wearing a nice pair of khaki shorts and a plain green T-shirt. My face was zitless, and my sneakers were clean. It was my hair that was not cooperating. It was sticking up more than usual, and there was nothing I could do about it.

Suddenly, I had an idea. My mom kept a can of non-aerosol hair spray in her bathroom that she used for "special occasions"—author lunches, conferences, cocktail parties. Surely hair spray—even the safe-for-the-environment non-aerosol kind—would help me with my hair.

I tiptoed through my parents' bedroom to their bathroom. The hair spray was sitting by itself next to the sink, as if waiting for me to take it. I picked it up and started back to my room. Unfortunately, in the hallway I bumped into my mother, who was carrying a basket of laundry. The hair spray flew out of my hands and landed neatly in front of her on top of Dad's jeans in the laundry basket.

We both studied the can silently for a few seconds. "Everything all right, Jackie?" Mom finally asked.

"Yeah," I said, trying to sound as casual as possible. "Everything's fine. Why do you ask?" I plastered a smile onto my face.

Mom snorted. "What would you possibly need with my hair spray?"

I kept on smiling. "My shoes need to be cleaned," I stammered. "I, uh, read somewhere that hair spray really does the trick." I nodded vigorously as if to drive home this point.

"I see," Mom replied, examining my unruly hair. "So you need my hair spray for your shoes."

"Uh-huh," I said stupidly, still nodding my head.

"Not your . . . hair?"

"Oh no," I replied. "Not at all." My smile was beginning to hurt my face. I couldn't tell my mom that I needed her hair spray for my hair because then I'd have to tell her about Kelly. I really didn't want to tell her about Kelly.

She'd make a big deal out of it—Kelly being my first-ever girlfriend—and who knows what weirdness would result. She might want to bless our relationship with herb potions or something.

"Just the same, I think I'll help you use the spray on your hair," she said.

"I can do it by myself," I answered, then quickly added, "I mean, I can do it on my shoes by myself."

Mom smirked. She carried the laundry basket, with the can of hair spray still in it, back to her bedroom, set the basket down on the floor, picked up the can, and motioned for me to come in.

I groaned. "Mom, really, I can do it," I protested.

She didn't reply. She made me come into the bathroom and stand in front of the mirror as she worked on my hair with a brush and the spray. It didn't take long. Before I knew it, she was done and my hair looked good.

"How's that—better?" she asked.

"Yeah," I admitted.

"You don't have to keep things to yourself all the time," she said. "You know that, right?"

"Um, yeah," I said, feeling uncomfortable.

"I can help sometimes, you know," she continued. "For instance, I'm a pro with hair spray. I bet you didn't know that."

"I know," I said.

"I'm a pro at other things, too," she said, "so don't be shy."

I briefly considered telling my mom everything that was on my mind—the double date, Cyrus the Virus, my failure of a novel.

"You ever feel," I began awkwardly, "that you can't do anything right, no matter how hard you try?"

Mom's face softened. "Failure is a part of life," she said quietly. "The important thing is not to give up. To figure out what you're doing wrong, change that, and keep at it."

"Uh, that's what I thought, too," I said, backing out of the room. I really didn't want to talk about it. I wished I hadn't said anything.

Mom seemed to sense this. "Drop by my salon anytime," she called out after me.

"I will," I answered as cheerfully as possible. I checked my watch. If I didn't leave now, I'd be late. I once again took a quick look in my mirror, then ran downstairs and raced out the door.

I rounded the corner hurriedly, finally reaching Nick's house. His parents were out again, and that meant something stupid was going to happen, but I hoped this time it wouldn't—especially to me, especially with Kelly Phillips there.

I rang the doorbell and tried to calm my racing heart. Nick came to the door. His hair was slicked back, and he was dressed as nicely as I've ever seen him. "Hello, Jackie," he said politely, and it was almost like he was a different person. "Welcome to your double date."

"Hi, Nick," I replied absently.

At that moment, Charlene appeared behind him. She looked more beautiful than ever. "Hey, Kelly!" she called behind her. "Your boyfriend's here!" She turned to me and smiled. "Hi, Jackie," she said sweetly.

"Hi," I replied, but I was too absorbed with the words "your boyfriend" to say anything else. She called me Kelly's boyfriend! *I* was Kelly Phillips's boyfriend!

Kelly came to the door, and as soon as I stepped inside,

she put her arms around me and kissed me loudly on the mouth. "I missed you," she said.

"I missed you, too," I said, feeling dizzy.

"Aren't they cute?" Charlene said to Nick after Kelly had finally let me go. "They're so in love."

"No, I'm the one who's in love," Nick said, and Charlene broke into delighted giggles. I thought I was going to gag. What did a girl like Charlene see in a guy like Nick? I wondered.

Nick led us all into the living room. There was a bottle of Coke on the coffee table, as well as a plate of chocolate chip cookies.

"Oh, Nickie," Charlene said with a pouty smile, "I can't have chocolate. I'm allergic." She pointed to the cookies, which were lumpy and irregular, a sure sign Nick had spent much of the day making them. He wouldn't be caught dead in the kitchen, unless it was for Charlene.

Nick smiled smoothly. "Never fear, darling," he said, and I wished I had a vomit bag with me because this time I really wanted to gag. "I'll be right back." He took her hands in his, kissed them, then left the living room.

Charlene looked at me with glittering eyes. "Your friend is such a gentleman," she gushed, "like a knight in shining armor," and I had to bite my lip to keep from cracking up.

"Yeah, you're right about that," I said as seriously as I could.

Nick returned with a second plate of lumpy, irregular cookies that he proclaimed were peanut butter. He passed the plate to Charlene and Kelly first, then to me. I was feeling too nervous to eat anything, but I took a cookie out of politeness and held it in my hand like an idiot.

We sat down facing each other, and Kelly and I watched Nick feed Charlene peanut butter cookies. I tried to imagine feeding Kelly a cookie and almost fainted at the thought of it. I could just see it: lifting the cookie in my hand—which by now would be warm and sticky—and gently pushing it into her beautiful mouth, watching her chew it seductively. . . .

I stopped and looked around. Kelly was staring at me, and I realized I had been smiling like a moron, with my eyes closed, as I imagined the cookie scene.

"What are you doing?" she asked.

"Nothing," I mumbled, feeling like a nitwit. I lowered my eyes and shoved the cookie into my mouth. I struggled to chew it, hoping I wouldn't spit it up in front of her. It actually tasted good.

Nick pulled a videotape out of a drawer. "I rented this for today," he announced. It was a movie about three German shepherds in Alaska.

Charlene clapped her hands. "I just love German shepherds," she exclaimed.

"Me, too," Nick lied, giving me a warning look.

Nick didn't need to worry—I wasn't going to blow his dog cover. I had more important things on my mind, such as deciding whether to put my arm around Kelly during the movie and trying to find out what French kissing was without asking anyone.

Nick turned on the movie. During the course of the film, he stopped it a few times to feed Charlene more cookies, pour her soda—he would have washed her feet if she asked. She was the royalty, and he was the servant. Of course, with a girl as beautiful and sweet as Charlene, maybe any other guy would do the same. But it seemed like the things that most mattered to her—dogs—were not going to be important to Nick anytime soon.

Kelly, meanwhile, had put her hand on my knee, and throughout the film, the spot where her hand lay kept getting hotter and hotter until I was sure her hand was going to burn through my skin. I wanted to put my arm around her, but I was afraid to move. In fact, after sitting without moving for two hours, I felt completely stiff.

There were several parts in the movie when the camera zoomed in on the dogs, and several times I could see Nick flinch slightly, then recover as quickly as possible. Charlene didn't seem to notice.

During the last scene of the movie, Kelly leaned toward me. I faced her and suddenly felt something warm and wet in my mouth. When she pulled away, I realized it was her tongue. Was this French kissing? I looked over at Nick and saw that he was staring at me. I was too shocked to do anything but watch a mangy-looking llama being chased by the dogs as the credits rolled.

After the movie we ate more cookies and drank more soda. Then Charlene suggested we play a word game— Doggy Names. We started with the letter A and went through the alphabet, taking turns thinking of a dog name for each letter, but it couldn't be a real name or a food or a plant.

The game was going pretty well. I had offered Doom for D, Horror for H, and Lie for L, when the girls announced they were going to the bathroom. They got up, leaving Nick and me alone in the living room. I was glad Kelly had left so I could move my stiffened body.

Nick was furious. "What are you doing, man?" he demanded.

"What do you mean?"

"What's with the dog names you're picking? You trying to curse me or something?"

"Huh?"

"Doom, Horror, Lie, Fake—"

"I didn't have *F*, Kelly did."

Nick sighed. "If you're trying to give me away with some smart writer word trick, it's not going to work, Hemingway."

"I wasn't trying—"

"It's not going to work," he repeated, but he looked worried.

"I wasn't trying to do anything," I said. I was shocked that Nick thought I would try to ruin his relationship with Charlene and flattered that he thought I had some kind of magical writer power to curse him through a dog game. But I guess he was right—I was picking names that sounded suspicious.

"How are the dog lessons going?" I asked sincerely.

He turned away. "Garus isn't, like, as interested as he was before."

"Huh?"

Nick stared at me with anger in his eyes—or was it hurt? "He's, like, less interested in doing things now."

"Really?" I asked in surprise. Garus was trying to break away from Nick, his hero? What would he do all by himself? Before I could complete this thought, Kelly and Charlene's footsteps sounded in the hall.

Nick confided, "I don't need him anyway. I've got Charlene now." He winked at me.

After the girls returned, Kelly placed her hand in position on my knee, and I took up the position of a corpse once more. I hoped we'd French kiss again, but it didn't happen. We continued the Doggy Names game through the letter Z, then went back through the alphabet again. I tried to pick noncursing names for my dogs and managed to succeed.

At the end of the game, Charlene asked Nick why he didn't have a dog since he loved them so much, and Nick stammered, "Oh, we had, like, five dogs last year, baby, but . . . they all died."

"They *all* died?" Charlene asked in a stunned whisper.

"All of them?" Kelly asked.

Nick nodded his head solemnly. "They were in my brother's car. He was taking them to the park. A truck hit him. He was O.K., but the dogs . . . they didn't make it."

"How horrible," Charlene said. Her eyes glistened, and I suddenly felt angry at Nick for putting her through this nonsense. As if reading my mind, he shot me a warning glance.

"What kind of dogs were they?" Charlene asked in tears.

Nick hesitated, and I wondered if he was about to say German shepherds, but even he probably knew how outlandish that would sound. "They were mutts," he said mournfully. "All mutts."

"Oh no, not mutts," Charlene cried, falling into his arms and sobbing.

It was hard, but I managed to keep my mouth shut.

At last, Charlene's dad came to get the girls. Charlene had recovered somewhat by then, and I could tell she felt that she and Nick shared a true dog bond now.

Kelly kissed me again—tongue and everything—and I think I blacked out for about three seconds. Then she

101

winked at me, and like a moron I tried winking back, except that I don't know how to wink, so she probably thought I had a twitch in my eye.

After they left, Nick seized me by the shirt and growled, "If you ever tell her I made up that story, Hemingway, I will personally kill you."

I told him I wouldn't and meant it. Anyway, I had a feeling the truth would come out by itself. It always does.

Chapter 15

> "It wasn't the first time I found a severed head in my trash can, but it was the first time I recognized it."

The double date had set me back a few days, because all I could think about was Kelly's tongue in my mouth and her hand on my knee, so I wasn't getting much writing done.

"I miss you," she had said today on the phone.

"Me, too," I replied, my shaking hand holding the receiver.

"When can I see you?" she asked.

I blurted out stupidly, "Want to come over?"

"Sure!" she exclaimed.

And so, here it was only a couple of hours before Kelly Phillips—the most beautiful girl in all of Frog Hollow—was supposed to come over to my house. I had cleaned up everything in the house, even the clothing pile in my room. (Actually, I just shoved the pile in my closet.) Mom and

Dad had left for a meeting of the Nutritionists Assembly. To prevent myself from thinking about Kelly, I thought I'd write. Who was I kidding? I couldn't write at all. I called Nick instead.

"Kelly's coming over," I croaked.

"I've got just the thing for you," he replied mysteriously.

A few minutes later, he and Garus showed up on my doorstep.

I opened the front door. Nick greeted me with a huge grin on his face. "This is your lucky day, Hemingway," he said.

"Congratulations are in order, old boy," Garus added. When he saw the confusion on my face, he explained, "On having your young lady pay you a visit."

Nick turned to him with annoyance. "Garus, will you ever talk normal?"

Garus studied him indignantly. "There is nothing improper about my speech," he replied. "Nothing improper whatsoever." He lifted his chin. "You'll miss it someday," he muttered.

Nick shook his head. Then he turned to me and patted his back pocket. "I got something to show you, Hemingway," he said. "It's going to be very useful to you today."

They both smiled fiendishly. We went up to my room, and Nick shut the door. He motioned to Garus. At his signal, Garus pulled two chairs from across the room and placed them in front of Nick. He was grinning madly.

"What are you guys up to?" I asked.

"Just watch and learn," Nick said, winking at me. From

his pocket he brought out a brassiere and wrapped it around one chair. "I give you, Hemingway, a bra."

My eyes nearly popped out of my head. "Where'd you get that?" I mumbled stupidly, my ears turning red.

Nick ignored my question, smiling at my embarrassment. "This is a delicate maneuver, Hemingway, so watch carefully," he said, clearly enjoying himself.

Garus and I watched, transfixed, as Nick sat down in the chair beside the one with the bra. He casually draped his arm around its top. Then he slid his hand down and deftly fingered the attachments in the back and the bra fell apart.

"Wow," Garus and I said in unison.

We each took our turn at the thing. It wasn't nearly as easy as Nick had made it look. The top hook was the hardest.

We kept up our bra work for a while, until we had it down to a science, giving in to Nick's vivid descriptions of what might occur if one could master such a handy talent.

Suddenly I realized the time. "Oh my God!" I cried. "She's going to be here any minute!"

Nick hurriedly stuffed the bra into his pocket while Garus put the two chairs back. They raced down the stairs just as a car pulled into our driveway. I could clearly make out Coach at the wheel as I opened the front door.

"I hope he doesn't stay to chaperone," Nick whispered to me, then hurried off with Garus trailing behind him. I shuddered at the thought.

I stood stupidly on the porch as Kelly kissed her father good-bye and got out of the car. I could swear Coach scowled at me before he backed out of the driveway and drove off.

Kelly walked slowly to the porch. "Hi," she said.

"Hi," I answered, my heart beating a mile a minute. For a moment, I didn't think I could go through with this date. I could just see the headlines: Boy Drops Dead on Porch. Lovesickness Kills Teen Novelist. Promising Young Author Succumbs to Love Disease.

"Jackie, didn't you hear me?" Kelly said loudly.

"What?" I looked at her. She had her hands on her hips. "Sorry, I must have zoned out," I said apologetically.

"Well, don't zone out," she said, stamping her foot. "I said I'm thirsty."

"Sorry," I said again, then felt seized with fear. I should have planned for this, because the only drinks we were likely to have in the fridge were soy milk and guava nectar. I don't think Kelly had soy milk and guava nectar in mind when she asked for a drink. More likely she assumed I lived in a normal household where people drank Coke and iced tea.

"Well?" she asked impatiently.

"Uh, sure, no problem," I stammered. I opened the door and let her in. Kelly sat on a sofa in the living room while I headed into the kitchen. I stood at the fridge trying to decide what to do when I heard a car pull into the garage.

"Jackie, we're home," Mom called as she opened the garage door. My body stiffened. They weren't supposed to be home for another three hours!

Mom and Dad walked into the kitchen. Mom absently kissed the top of my head. "Hi, sweetie," she said.

"You're early!" I blurted out, causing them both to eye me sharply.

"Phil wasn't feeling well," Dad explained. Phil was one of

106

the weirdest guys on the planet and the president of the Assembly.

"I told him to cut down on all that flaxseed he's been eating," Mom said. She tsked tsked. Dad nodded sympathetically.

I must have looked clearly horrified because Mom asked, "Is something wrong, sweetheart?"

"Uh, uh," I stammered.

"You feeling O.K.?" Dad asked with concern. "You seem a little flushed."

Mom put her hand on my forehead. "You do feel warm," she said. "Let me take your temperature."

"No!" I cried. "I gotta, uh, go somewhere right now."

"Oh, the novel can wait," Mom said impatiently. "This will only take a minute." She opened a drawer and pulled out a thermometer.

"I'm fine," I protested. "I gotta go. Really."

"Jackie, this will only take a minute. Sit down," she commanded.

I had no choice but to sit down as Mom tucked a thermometer under my tongue. At that instant, with Mom and Dad hovering over me and talking about their freak assembly, Kelly walked into the kitchen.

"Uh, hi. I heard you in here," she explained awkwardly.

Mom and Dad froze, eyeing her with a mixture of shock and delight, then looked at me for an explanation.

"Tdhis isd Kellyd Phillipsd," I said before realizing I still had the thermometer in my mouth.

"I'm Jackie's girlfriend," Kelly said helpfully.

Mom's eyes grew round. "You have a girlfriend?" she asked in disbelief. Kelly giggled, and I thought I was going to die.

107

"It's nice to meet you," Dad said, shaking Kelly's hand. He turned to me with a huge smile on his face. "Way to go," he mouthed silently, and for the second time, I thought I was going to die.

What Mom said next, though, truly had the potential to send me to an early grave. "Well, you'll have to stay for dinner," she exclaimed merrily.

"Um, O.K.," Kelly said politely.

Mom turned to Dad. "Let's invite Cerise. We'll make this into a big thing!"

No—not Cerise!

She turned to me excitedly. "And we'll cook that new soy chicken I bought," she said, more to herself than to me. "And we'll have lemon-grass sauce and couscous with vegetables and. . . ."

"How about pizza?" I asked desperately. I knew they'd never consider ordering one, but at least my mom's vegetarian pizza was edible.

Mom looked at me as if I'd slapped her. "Pizza!" she said contemptuously, as if it were the vilest substance on earth. "Absolutely not. This is an occasion that deserves more than *pizza*.

"Now, you two run along, and we'll call you when dinner's ready," she went on, consumed with her dinner plans. She made a shooing motion with her hands.

Kelly and I trudged upstairs to my room. I had a terrible feeling that this dinner was going to be a total disaster—and wouldn't you know it—I was 100 percent right.

We spent the next hour hanging out in my room. I soon ran out of things to talk about, and Kelly didn't seem interested in French kissing. The only exciting thing that happened was when she asked me if I had any secrets in my closet. I thought of my clothing pile but decided against showing it to her. I could just see her opening the door and my clothes tumbling out, smothering her in an avalanche of T-shirts, shorts, jeans, and socks. She would suffocate, and I'd be arrested for manslaughter. I could see the headlines: Boy Kills Girl with His Clothes. Teen Sentenced to Life Imprisonment in Apparel Case. Dead Girl's Father Vows Revenge. That last one gave me the shivers.

"No secrets in there," I said with a nervous laugh.

"What are those?" Kelly asked, pointing at my fishtank.

"Goldfish."

Kelly made a face. "Fish are slimy. They're gross."

For someone who spent a lot of time in water, she had strange views about fish. Mark Twain, Isaac Asimov, and Dashiell Hammett were *not* slimy. Or gross. "I named them after my favorite writers," I explained. "You see, I'm writing a—"

"Dogs are much better pets than fish," Kelly interrupted, then immersed herself in examining her fingernails. I watched her silently. I guess I could see her point, but why compare fish and dogs? There was really nothing to compare. One was wet and silent, the other was frisky and furry. Besides, Dad was allergic to dogs. That's why we didn't have one. I was about to say something along those lines when Mom and Dad called us down. I was almost glad. I looked at my watch. Six o'clock on the dot. Without much enthusiasm, we trudged downstairs.

In the dining room, the table was set nicely enough. There were even flowers from the garden for a centerpiece.

Mom and Dad were buzzing over everything like headwaiters at a busy restaurant, and I could tell Kelly was a little embarrassed by all the fuss they were making.

I was beginning to think things might go well after all, until Cerise showed up. She rang the doorbell three times to ward off evil spirits. The number three had magical powers, she always said. Mom let her in and gave her a big hug. Then Dad hugged her, too. Finally she came into the dining room.

"My, how lovely everything looks," she said in a deep, husky voice. Then she turned to us and said the thing I was most dreading. "The body knows." She patted her rump three times.

I turned to Kelly. Her mouth had dropped open.

Cerise walked right up to her. She was wearing a purple dress that came down to her ankles, and her black hair spilled out of a matching purple beret. She had a big mole on her chin and a mustache on her upper lip. All in all, she looked like a witch. But she was my parents' best-selling author.

Cerise reached out to touch Kelly on the cheek, but Kelly took a step backward. It didn't seem to faze Cerise. Maybe she was used to people doing that. "Who is this lovely child?" she asked.

Kelly's mouth was still wide open, and I could tell she wasn't going to answer the question. So I said, "This is Kelly. Kelly Phillips."

Cerise turned to me as if seeing me for the first time. "Kelly Phillips," she repeated. Then she said, "Jackie, you look good enough to eat." She bared her teeth at me. I flinched—I couldn't help it. Then she smiled, and I could hear it coming from a mile away. "The body knows," she said, as if she hadn't already said it, and wouldn't be saying it another zillion times before the end of the night. She patted her rump three times.

By now Kelly had closed her mouth, but she had an extremely disturbed expression on her face. Mom and Dad did not seem to notice. Mom said cheerily, "Well, let's start. Cerise, you sit there. Jackie and Kelly, over there."

We took our seats. Kelly stared into her lap. Cerise said, "Allow me to say a prayer for our well-being." We bowed our heads as Cerise chanted something in another language and ended by saying, "The wizards are watching over us tonight. The body knows."

"Amen," Mom and Dad said together.

I peeked at Kelly. She looked like she was going to cry.

Mom passed around plates of soy chicken, couscous with vegetables, lemon-grass sauce, sprout salad, and oat-bran rolls. As I studied the inedible food, and Cerise drooling over it, and Mom and Dad oblivious to the weirdness of everything, and Kelly's obvious discomfort at all this, I couldn't help thinking that I had somehow been transported into an episode of *The Twilight Zone*.

"Kelly, angel, how old are you?" Cerise asked with a mouth full of sprouts.

Kelly grimaced. "I'm thirteen," she said quietly.

Cerise's eyes grew round. "Thirteen!" she exclaimed, and three sprouts flew out of her mouth, landing on the oat-bran rolls. "Thirteen is the age of mystical wonders," she said, nodding her huge head three times. "Mystical wonders," she repeated, then said, of course, "The body knows." A sprout was hanging out of the side of her mouth, and I had the urge to pull it out and stab her with it.

Kelly looked at me. I smiled helplessly. She frowned miserably at her plate, tentatively pushing around the food with her fork, then stabbed a piece of soy chicken and brought it to her mouth. She chewed carefully, stopped abruptly, reached for her water glass, and drank it down in one gulp.

"More water?" I asked stupidly. She smiled wanly and nodded.

"Cerise has written five books," Dad said to us between bites of couscous. "And they've all been bestsellers."

Mom nodded. "She's quite a talented woman."

Kelly sighed, and I stared at her plate. She hadn't tried anything since the bite of soy chicken. Everyone else was finished. I was about to suggest something radical, like being excused so we could get salami sandwiches from my private stash, when Cerise said, "Let's all recite the ancient circle of prayers."

Mom and Dad nodded enthusiastically. Kelly glanced at me pleadingly.

"You'll like this," Cerise told her, then added, "The body knows," as I winced.

But Kelly lasted for only five minutes of the ancient circle of prayers. Right in the middle of the Prayer of Paneer, she complained of not feeling well. She called home. Coach came and got her, and she didn't even kiss me good-bye.

And so, I was left alone with my parents and Cerise and the ancient circle of prayers. When the prayers finally ended and Mom announced dessert—Dad's famous squash-flower pudding—I decided I'd had enough. I went up to my room and right to bed, trying to forget that the evening had ever happened.

Chapter 16

❝He was born at home, but when his mother saw him, she went to the hospital.❞

Humor—now there's a great genre for a novel. It's too bad I had to leave early for the swim club. I would've cranked out a whole chapter for sure.

Today was our long-awaited swim meet against Brewster. As I walked to the swim club, I found myself getting revved up to beat them. I just hoped Cyrus the Virus would be too busy to beat me up.

When I arrived, the first thing that caught my eye was a cluster of girls gathered around Kelly by the snack bar. They were all laughing and shaking their heads in unison at something she was telling them—it was obviously very funny. As I got closer she dramatically patted her rump three times. A small voice in the back of my mind tried to warn me, but I ignored it and swaggered up to her in my best Nick imitation.

"Hey there," I said in a deep voice.

The girls stopped laughing and stared at me. Then they broke into laughter again. Kelly laughed the loudest. "What's so funny?" I asked, but that only made them laugh harder.

After what seemed like hours, the other girls finally left, and it was just me and Kelly standing there by ourselves. She had a smirk on her face that made me gulp loudly with fear.

"What's up, beautiful?" I asked anxiously.

She rolled her eyes, and my stomach suddenly tightened.

"Is something wrong?" I asked, hoping she'd say no and kiss me.

Kelly looked down at her sneaker. "There's something I gotta tell you," she said.

I waited, shifting my weight nervously from one foot to the other.

"I don't think this is working," she said matter-of-factly, still looking down. "I think we should break up."

It took a few seconds for her words to hit me. "Break up?" I asked in disbelief.

She nodded, then turned away.

For a minute, neither of us spoke. "Why?" I finally asked.

Kelly looked at me with annoyance. "We're just too different," she said, shrugging her shoulders. "Your family is so . . . weird."

Whatever excitement I had felt about beating Brewster began leaking out of me like a deflating balloon. "But—" I began, not knowing what to say. I wasn't weird! It was my parents and their business and Cerise. . . .

"I don't want to talk about it," she interrupted coldly. "I gotta go," she said, looking beyond me, and walked away.

She left me standing there for I don't know how long. I would have stood there all day if Coach hadn't blown his whistle. Obediently, I lined up at the edge of the pool, though I was in shock and didn't hear a word he was saying.

Cyrus was standing on the other side of the pool. I gulped, but he wasn't paying any attention to me. He was talking to Kelly. She patted him on the arm. They both suddenly turned and stared at me. Cyrus made a cutting motion across his throat. Kelly laughed. I felt my entire body go limp.

The rest of the morning passed in a blur. I remember seeing Garus and Nick, I remember the other goons from Brewster, I even remember the race that I swam, but that's all. By the end of the meet, I was totally out of it.

Brewster killed us 90 to 61.

After the meet was over and Brewster had left, Coach lined us up at the pool and walked silently up and down the line, looking up every once in a while with a disgusted expression on his face. He dismissed us without saying a word. I followed Garus and Nick to the snack bar, my mind still in a fog.

Nick and Garus each ordered a cheeseburger. I wasn't hungry, so I just sat there staring into space, my mind replaying what Kelly had said to me. Suddenly, a kid with terrible acne came up to me and said, "Coach wants to see you."

Before I had a chance to respond, another snotty-nosed kid came up to me and dutifully repeated the message. "Coach wants to see you."

I glared at Garus and Nick and wondered if they were playing a cruel prank on me.

"Are you guys playing with me?" I asked them.

Nick looked up from his cheeseburger. "What are you talking about?"

"What's this about then?" I asked.

Nick shrugged. "I dunno," he said absently, turning back to his cheeseburger.

Garus wiped his mouth carefully with a napkin. "Gentlemen," he said, "I'm going to the loo."

Nick scowled at him, then chomped down on his burger. I decided I had to find out for myself what was going on.

Garus walked beside me, heading toward the bathroom as I approached Coach, who was talking to Stinky. I walked boldly up to him and said, "I heard you wanted to see—"

"GET IN MY OFFICE!"

I did an about-face and headed toward his office.

Garus looked at me with concern. "Was he talking to me, too?"

"I don't know," I said miserably. "Ask him."

Garus approached Coach, who was still deep in conversation with Stinky. Before Garus could say a word, Coach turned in his direction and bellowed, "I THOUGHT I TOLD YOU TO GET IN MY OFFICE!"

It struck me then that in our swim-team bathing suits, sunglasses, and baseball caps, Garus and I looked exactly alike. Well, it was too late to do anything about it.

We both walked into the supply room that doubled as Coach's office. Dust-covered file cabinets, topped by various swimming paraphernalia, stood against the walls. There was a lone desk and chair in the center of the room. We sat on the floor.

We soon heard Coach's voice in the distance, and to my surprise, I got giant goose bumps on my arms and legs. He barged in, not even looking at us. He sat down at the desk and started shuffling some papers. He then glanced up and seemed startled. I can only guess that it was because he saw two swimmers instead of one.

"You swam like ninnygoats today," he said.

I could sort of understand what a "ninnygoat" was, but I wanted to be sure. I opened my mouth to ask, but then thought better of it.

"Don't you want to win?"

Garus and I were silent.

Coach drew himself up to his full height and bellowed, "I SAID, DON'T YOU WANT TO WIN?"

"Yes, sir!" We both shouted together.

"GET OUT THERE AND DO YOUR LAPS!" he screamed.

We both got up and, resisting the temptation to run, slowly walked out. Kids came rushing to us from all directions. "Did he hit you?" they asked.

"No!" we said about ten times.

The rest of the day was spent in an exhausting repetition of laps. I noticed Kelly with her girlfriends at the snack bar and quickly turned away. When the end of the miserable day finally arrived, I was about to head home and collapse when the same acne-faced kid came up to me and said, "Coach wants to see you."

Oh, man.

"Coach wants to see you," a freckle-faced kid informed me a minute later.

I saw Coach in the distance and casually walked up to him. "Did you want to see—"

"GET IN MY OFFICE!"

I did an about-face and walked into his office. I sat on the floor and stared at the same dust-covered file cabinets. The place was becoming a home away from home.

Coach came in and didn't even look at me. He sat down at the desk and shuffled the same papers. Without turning to me, he said, "We have to beat Brewster next time."

What was I supposed to say? I moved my mouth, but nothing came out.

He turned to me, his eyes filled with anger. "I'm counting on you, Monterey."

"Yeah," I muttered stupidly, my voice sounding strange to me.

"I've been watching you, boy," he went on. "Watching closely." He leaned forward menacingly. "You better know it," he said.

It suddenly occurred to me that the reason Coach called me in here was to tell me he was sick of seeing his daughter waste her time with a loser like me.

"We broke up!" I blurted out. Then I said quietly, "She dumped me."

For a minute, Coach studied me silently. "I know that," he finally said, looking amused. "But that's not what I'm talking about, boy." He rose from his desk and walked over to me. "That's not what I meant at all," he said in a softer voice. "I've been watching you because you've got something, boy," he said, making a fist with his hand. "You're misguided, that's all. You're on the wrong track. I want to put you on the right track."

He went back to his desk and sat down. "You've got what it takes, boy." He pounded the table with his fist, making me jump. "You just need help to make it happen."

I couldn't have understood it then, but Coach had hit the nail right on the head. He was talking about more than just swimming, of course. Only I didn't know it at the time. So when I just sat there, trying to make sense of his little speech to me, the next thing he said made me jump about five feet in the air.

"GET OUT THERE AND DO YOUR LAPS!"

I scrambled up, tripped, fell, then got up again and ran out. The club was nearly empty, but I dove into the pool and started swimming. Coach walked out of his office and stood at the pool's edge with his arms folded, watching me silently. He called me over mid-lap and crouched down next to me.

"Your strokes are too choppy," he said. "Follow through more."

I didn't know what he meant, but I tried to make my strokes longer.

Again in mid-lap he stopped me. "Extend more when you kick out," he said. Again I tried to do what he said. I don't know if it was his advice, but I suddenly noticed that I was moving faster through the water.

Coach stopped me four more times, each time giving me a new order. By the time I hauled myself out of the pool, I was exhausted. But he was right—I *was* swimming better.

"Nice work, Monterey," he said gruffly, and despite myself, I felt a glow inside. I left the swim club tired but feeling better.

When I walked into the house, I only wanted to fall into bed, but instead I was greeted by a tall, bearded man with a colorful snake around his neck.

"Hi," the man said, stroking the snake nonchalantly.

"Uh . . . hi," I replied, quickly taking three steps back.

He looked at me with half-closed eyes. "I'm Copperhead," he said.

"Excuse me?"

"You must be John Jr."

"Jackie," I corrected.

"It's such a pleasure to meet you," he said morosely.

Just then my mother sailed in, struggling with a giant stack of papers.

"Oh, hi, honey," she chirped in my direction, adjusting the stack in her arms. "I see you've met Copperhead and Larry."

I snorted. Larry was the *snake*, and Copperhead was the *owner*. Figures.

"Let me help you with that," Copperhead said. He took the papers from Mom with his right hand and continued stroking Larry with his left hand.

"You're such a pretty snake, aren't you?" Mom cooed, reaching her hand out toward Larry. Larry, who had been regarding us all coolly, hissed and shot a forked tongue out at my mother. She recoiled her hand quickly, then cleared her throat.

"Well, Copperhead, shall we go into the office?"

"Yes, that would be magnificent," Copperhead replied with a glum sigh.

"Copperhead is writing a book about the healing power of pythons," Mom said to me excitedly. She must have been able to tell what I thought about that, because she turned away swiftly and said, "Well, right this way, Copperhead."

"It was lovely to meet you, Jackie," Copperhead said sullenly.

"Yeah, me too," I said as Mom ushered Copperhead and Larry away. "The healing power of pythons?" I asked myself aloud.

I wanted to feel angry that a man with a snake was walking around my house. I wanted to feel angry that the reason Kelly broke up with me—and all her girlfriends laughed at me—was that my parents were so weird. I wanted to feel angry about everything—my novel, Brewster, Cyrus the Virus—but I was too damn tired. So I went to bed, and only then did I realize that Coach had planned it that way.

Chapter 17

> ❝He wiped the blade with his handkerchief, taking care not to spill the blood.❞

A novel about a guy who kills the girl who breaks his heart seemed appropriate right now, but I didn't have much of a plot beyond the opening line. I turned to Mark, Isaac, and Dashiell, who were swimming placidly in their tank without a care in the world. "Whatever you do, guys, don't ever get mixed up with girl fish," I told them.

For the next hour I just sat there thinking about Kelly and what she had done to me. How could a girl who was so beautiful be so cruel? I was feeling so bad about it that when the doorbell rang, I was almost hoping it was Nick and Garus. And it was. I opened the door and stood with them on the front porch.

"Heard about what happened," Nick said soberly. "Bad scene, Hemingway."

"Yeah," I said, marveling at how quickly the news had traveled.

Garus was holding a plate covered with foil. He handed it to me with a flourish. "They're English scones," he said proudly. "I baked them to lighten your misfortune, old boy."

"What the hell are scones?" Nick asked irritably.

Garus looked at him as if he'd just asked the dumbest question on earth. "They're like biscuits," he replied curtly. "You eat them at teatime with Devonshire cream and jam."

Nick shook his head, no doubt thinking Garus was taking this English thing too far. I agreed, but I appreciated his thoughtfulness. "Thanks, Garus," I said sincerely.

"No trouble at all, old chap," he said with a grin.

Nick rolled his eyes and took his comb out. "Dames," he said to me, running the comb briskly through his hair. "You don't need 'em, Hemingway."

"Yeah, I guess not," I said without enthusiasm.

"You're better off," he went on.

"Yeah." I didn't agree, but what else could I say? "Do you guys want to come inside?" I asked.

"Nah," Nick answered. "We gotta take the dogs out for a walk." He jerked his thumb in Garus's direction.

"The dog lessons are back?" I asked, glancing at Garus.

Garus lowered his eyes. "Unfortunately," he muttered under his breath.

Nick didn't seem to hear him. "Wouldn't you for Charlene?" He made a motion with his hands indicating her figure. "Oops. Sorry, Hemingway."

I hung my head.

"You're better off," he said again. Then he jabbed Garus

in the ribs. "Let's go," he said. "I gotta get that pooper-scooper part down."

I watched them go and sighed. Nick had Charlene and Mallory had Edgar. What did I have? Goldfish and salami? "This is one helluva bad scene," I said out loud.

I remained on the porch and noticed Mr. Conrad walking Fifi on the other side of the street. He was wearing an artist's smock splattered with yellow paint. He waved. I waved back. He crossed the street and stopped in front of the house.

"Hello, Jackie," he said pleasantly. "No more car-painting problems?"

"No," I said with a slight smile.

"Good to hear it," he replied.

I hesitated, then blurted out, "I've got girl problems now."

"Oh?"

I started telling Mr. Conrad about Kelly. Then I spilled my whole guts out about everything else from my lousy summer vacation. He listened quietly, nodding his head every so often.

"Kelly Phillips is the most beautiful girl in town," I said in conclusion.

Mr. Conrad rubbed his chin thoughtfully for a moment. "Yes, well," he said to himself, then looked up. "Sometimes appearances can be deceiving."

My face must have shown my confusion. "What?" I asked.

He studied me and said, "You say she was beautiful. But, did she take an interest in your novel, Jackie?"

The question startled me. "Uh, um," I stammered, remembering how Kelly had interrupted me when I tried telling her about it. "No," I said.

"Your fish?"

"No," I said.

"Your friends?"

"No."

Mr. Conrad smiled. "There, you see?"

I shook my head. "Uh, no," I said.

He frowned. "You mustn't be so rigid in your thinking, Jackie," he said.

"Um, I don't understand, Mr. Conrad."

"Kelly is beautiful, Edgar is a goon, your parents are weird, Nick and Garus do stupid things," he said. I marveled at how quickly he seemed to understand everything I'd told him.

"That kind of thinking is rigid," he went on. He gazed into my eyes. "See beyond it, Jackie. A writer must see beyond things." He looked away, then gazed into my eyes again. "You might even want to see beyond your novel."

As I stared at Mr. Conrad and tried to make sense of what he said, Fifi strained her leash toward home. Mr. Conrad smiled at her and said, "Think about it, Jackie." With that he walked off down the street.

"Rigid thinking?" I asked myself in bewilderment. "I don't know what he's talking about."

I sighed and reentered the house. When I got to the stairs, I stopped short. I really didn't want to spend the day sitting alone in my room with my typewriter, blank pieces of paper, and fish who didn't seem to care about anything except when the next batch of goldfish food was coming. I had been ignoring Mallory for weeks, ever since Kelly came into my life, but now I really needed her. I would head over there. And if Edgar the goon was with her, I'd tell him to leave.

I got dressed, choosing my clothes from the clothing pile in my closet, and headed out. As I walked toward Mallory's I tried again to figure out what Mr. Conrad told me, but for the life of me I couldn't make heads or tails of it. When I reached her house I decided to forget about it.

Mallory came to the door with a smile on her face. "Hi, m.p.," she said happily.

"Hi," I said, feeling a little better. I lowered my voice and asked, "Is Edgar here?"

"Not at the moment," Mallory answered in the same tone of voice.

I frowned, but she ignored me and opened the door. She led me to the kitchen table, where a stack of books about theme parks lay.

"Where'd you get those?" I asked as we sat down.

Mallory smiled. "Edgar brought them," she sang out.

I winced. "Where'd he get them?"

"I.h.g.a.c.," she said. (I haven't got a clue.)

I studied the books thoughtfully. "So Edgar's not a goon even though he's big and hangs out with Cyrus the Virus?" I asked.

Mallory glared at me.

"What?"

"No, he is not a goon," she said impatiently. "You're not a goon just because you're big. And I told you why he hangs out with Cyrus. They're cousins." She examined her fingernails—a sure sign that the subject should be dropped.

"How's the swim team?" she asked.

I frowned. "Well, I'm sure you heard what happened."

Mallory nodded. "You were too good for her, m.p.," she said curtly.

I coughed. It would be no use talking to Mallory about Kelly.

"How's your swimming?" she asked.

"It's pretty good," I said, then muttered, "Coach made, uh, some suggestions."

Mallory eyed me carefully. "That's a great start, m.p.," she said. "I'm proud of you," and I wondered what she meant by that. "How's your novel?" she asked next.

I hesitated, not knowing whether I should tell the truth or lie. I opted for a little of both. "Well, it's O.K., but not wonderful," I said cryptically.

She narrowed her eyes at me. "Still not following *their* suggestions, eh?" she asked. "Good old Mom and Dad?"

"I don't need their suggestions," I said defensively.

Mallory smiled. "If I remember correctly, you once said you were a 'great swimmer' and didn't need any swimming advice."

"That's different," I shot out, knowing it wasn't and feeling suddenly uncomfortable.

Mallory sighed. "Your stubbornness will be your downfall, m.p."

I stared at her. What was everyone talking about? Rigid, stubborn. . . . I shook my head. "My parents are weirdos, Mallory," I said. "They publish weird books. Their advice is worthless. Maybe if I was writing about pythons or chanting or—"

"They are not weirdos," Mallory interrupted. "They're just . . . ahead of their time."

I rolled my eyes. She was just brainwashed. We sat in silence for a few minutes.

Finally, Mallory said, "Look, Jackie, I know you don't want to ask your parents for advice, but at least listen to what they told you before. Write what you know. About your life."

"People wouldn't want to read about my life," I replied testily. "People want to read about space battles and serial murderers and cowboys. *Adventures*."

"You've had adventures, too," she said in a tone that sounded like an accusation.

"Adventures? What adventures?"

"What adventures?" she asked in disbelief. "The sewer pipe. The car painting. The hunt for *Playboy*."

I raised one eyebrow. Mallory smirked. "You've had *many* adventures," she insisted. "How did you spend your summer vacation, Jackie?"

"In the most boring way possible," I answered angrily.

She sighed as I got up to leave. "'A good writer can make anything sound interesting,'" she said, quoting from *GET RICH QUICK!*

"I guess I'm just not a good writer, then," I replied, without really meaning it.

"I guess not," Mallory said sadly.

Chapter 18

“Two X-Jowls climbed slowly out of the sewer pipe. Professor Sanford Herringbone and Faka Kulu studied them cautiously for a minute, then went back to painting the old car.”

So much for writing about my "adventures"—I knew it wouldn't work. At least I could say I wasn't being rigid—whatever everyone meant by that. Still, time wasn't on my side anymore. Frog Hollow Day was fast approaching, and that meant the summer was essentially over.

Frog Hollow Day was the third most important holiday in our town. On Frog Hollow Day, the whole town gathered on the green to celebrate Frog Hollow's founding in 1834. The town's founder was—who else?—Edwin J. Frog. Everyone thought Frog Hollow had something to do with frogs, but it didn't. It had everything to do with Edwin J. Frog.

Frog Hollow Day was a big fund-raising event, with proceeds going to the town recreation department, including the swim club. Which meant the swim team would be drafted into helping. Which meant the end of my writing career.

When the planning committee had its first volunteer meeting, Coach sent us all there to sign up. Mallory went the day before to get approval for her theme-park booth, which she put on every year. Mom and Dad went, too—to the dismay of the planning committee—to petition for a "holistic lifestyle" booth. Every year they went—and every year they were turned down.

But, to everyone's astonishment, after ten years of unsuccessfully petitioning the planning committee, Mom and Dad were given the go-ahead for their booth. It was a miracle! You see, Frog Hollow had never really accepted my parents. People in small towns generally don't like weirdness, and Frog Hollow is no exception. Luckily, I had always managed to fit in somehow. There were occasional nasty episodes, such as the time in fourth grade when a bully called me "yoga boy" and gave me a black eye. But, for the most part, I had very little trouble. My parents, however, had a rough time. But they never let town disapproval stop them. And now, their Frog Hollow Day booth was finally going to be a reality.

I couldn't help feeling a little proud, yet I shuddered to think what people would do when they saw the booth. If Kelly Phillips broke up with me after eating dinner with my parents, the town would probably lynch us once they saw their booth. I was pondering this as I walked to the Frog Hollow Community Center with Nick and Garus for the planning committee meeting.

Nick was frantically combing his hair, as usual. When he saw me looking at him, he winked. "I know what you're thinking, Hemingway," he said. "Don't ya worry. You won't have to go to Frog Hollow Day alone. Charlene and I'll set ya up with someone."

"I wasn't thinking about that," I said irritably. "And stop calling me Hemingway."

"You're a writer, aren't ya?" he asked innocently.

"No, I'm not," I said with a mixture of anger and despair. I *wish* I could have said, "Yes, I'm a writer. A novelist, to be exact." But I had let the whole summer pass with nothing to show for it but crumpled-up pieces of paper. Now Mom and Dad would be able to say once again, "You know, Jackie never finishes what he starts." Then they would say, "He should've just gone to Diamond Jubilee Computer Camp. The summer would've at least been productive."

I clenched my fists. Just because Frog Hollow Day was here didn't mean the summer was over. I still had a few days left. I was going to write something. I *was* going to write something.

"Sheesh, Hemingway, lighten up," Nick went on. "It's almost Frog Hollow Day!"

To Nick, Frog Hollow Day was the ultimate in babe satisfaction. There were rides and games and food, babes to meet, other kids from school to see and gossip with. Charlene was quite a prize to show off, and Nick knew it. No wonder the smile on his face was bigger than Texas. Garus, on the other hand, seemed peeved.

"I'm the one who loves dogs, you know," he muttered.

"What was that?" Nick asked.

"Nothing," Garus said with a sigh.

"Did you say something about dogs?"

"No, I did not, man," Garus answered with annoyance. He turned to me, then looked away. I shook my head sadly. Garus *was* the one who loved dogs.

At last we reached the community center. People filled the folding chairs set out in neat rows in the lobby. A lot of the swim-team guys were there. A long table was set up in front, where a group of ancient-looking people sat. Nick, Garus, and I chose three seats in the back row, which would prove to be a huge mistake.

Mrs. Elise Butterfield, the oldest citizen in Frog Hollow, suddenly hollered, "THIS MEETING WILL COME TO ORDER!" At once, the room fell silent. She looked around the room with a toothless smile, then turned to the geezer sitting next to her. "YOU MAY PROCEED, DICK!" she screamed at him.

Dick, who had covered his ears when Mrs. Butterfield addressed him, stood and gazed at each of us sourly.

"Thank you for coming," he said in a girlish-sounding voice, then gave a speech about how important Frog Hollow Day was to the town. Every so often his left eyebrow shot up unexpectedly, making everyone jump in their seats. After a while, I realized it happened on every seventh word, and everyone else must have, too, because they seemed to expect it, and we all jumped in unison. Because I was concentrating so hard on counting to seven, however, I didn't hear much of his speech.

"Depends . . . appreciate . . . money . . . day . . . fun . . . frogs . . . and . . . you," Dick said, then stopped, apparently finished. He grinned widely, his eyebrow shooting up twice in a row. Everyone clapped politely. He bowed four times, then sat down, still grinning.

Mrs. Butterfield smiled grotesquely at the warm reception her colleague had received. "WE WILL NOW GIVE OUT ASSIGNMENTS!" she shouted.

There was a low murmur in the room as everyone prepared to receive a job.

"SILENCE!" she screamed, and the room was instantly quiet. She squinted at a stack of papers in her hands.

"NI-CHO-LAS POS-IT-AN-O," she read.

I glanced at Nick. He quickly put away his comb. "Yo!" he said.

Mrs. Butterfield took a slow look around the room. "NI-CHO-LAS POS-IT-AN-O?"

Nick said, "Yo!" a little louder.

Mrs. Butterfield did another sweep of the room. "NI-CHO-LAS POS-IT-AN-O! IF YOU'RE HERE, SAY SO, FOR GOODNESS SAKE!"

Nick waved his arms madly, but Mrs. Butterfield had turned away.

"WHY DO THEY SIGN UP AND NOT SHOW?" she shouted irritably to Dick, who leaned as far away from her as possible.

"I'M RIGHT HERE!" Nick yelled, standing and waving his arms high above his head. His cheeks were bright red.

Mrs. Butterfield squinted hard and gazed at the back row for what seemed like hours. Then she put a hand above her eyes and stared some more. Finally, she stood up and leaned over the table.

"YOU'LL BE DOING FLOWER BASKETS," she said abruptly, turning back to her stack of papers.

"Flower baskets?" Nick mumbled.

Before Nick could say anything else, Mrs. Butterfield bellowed, "JOHN MONTEREY JR."

Desperately wanting to avoid the embarrassment that had befallen Nick, I was on my feet quickly, waving my arms SOS-style. "HERE!" I shouted.

"YOU'RE ON TABLE-SKIRT DUTY," she said in the same flat tone.

"JONATHAN BEN-JOSEPH."

Someone in the front row lifted a hand timidly. Mrs. Butterfield smiled upon him benevolently. "YOU'RE ON GARBAGE DUTY."

In the back, Garus and Nick snickered.

"GARY WHITE."

Garus jumped up and waved his arms furiously. "I AM PRESENT!" he yelled.

Mrs. Butterfield smiled again. "YOU'RE ON GARBAGE DUTY, TOO."

The snickering abruptly ceased.

Garus leaned over to me. "Jackie, old chap," he whispered, "would you consider a trade of sorts—"

"Forget it," I told him. He sighed, looking morose.

The meeting continued until everyone had received an assignment from Mrs. Butterfield. Then she banged her fist on the table and commanded, "YOU'RE DISMISSED. GO HOME!"

"Well, guys," Nick said, taking out his comb, "looks like we'll be busy in the next few days." He combed his hair furiously. I watched him, wondering for the first time why it didn't just fall out from so much handling. "Not much time to do anything else," he went on.

I let that thought sink in. As if reading my mind, he turned to me and asked, "Hey, how's your novel going?"

I didn't know what to say. "It's good," I lied.

He nodded absently. "When you're famous, Hemingway, we can say we knew you when you were doing table skirts!" He cracked up, and Garus joined in.

I watched the two of them silently, wishing the earth would open under my feet and swallow me up.

When I got home, Mom and Dad were in the midst of their own Frog Hollow Day preparations. Excitement about their booth hung over the house like a fog, overshadowing everything else. Mom had even canceled an editorial meeting with Copperhead in order to get organized.

"What if he gets mad and lets Larry loose in the house?" I protested.

"Oh, Jackie, honestly," Mom said with a disgusted expression on her face. She was standing in the middle of the living room holding a list the length of a roll of toilet paper.

I was serious. "But, Mom," I whined, "pythons are dangerous!"

Mom shook her head, refusing to let my fears of snake strangulation get in the way of her booth plans. Dad stood beside her inside a mountain of cardboard boxes and resembled a deer caught in car headlights.

"Pau D'Arco tea," Mom said, reading off the list.

"Uh, it's here somewhere," Dad said meekly.

"We've got to be organized, honey," Mom said firmly. "How about macadamia nut butter?"

"Check."

"Designer protein powder?"

"Check."

"Soy ice cream?"

"Check."

"Glycerine?"

"Check."

"Thirty copies of Ronald Hoffman's book?"

"Uh, I think we only have seventeen."

Frowning, Mom made a notation on her list.

I tiptoed through the boxes and went up to my room. Later that night, I had trouble sleeping. Finally, I got up and checked under my bed. There was no giant python coiled there, red eyes glowing evilly in the dark, ready to strangle me. I got back under the covers and sighed contentedly.

Chapter 19

66 The townspeople chanted in unison
as the helpless girl was
offered up to the Python God in sacrifice. 99

Having to be up at five o'clock in the morning did not leave me much time to write. That's right—I said five o'clock in the morning. That's when you have to be up when you're on table-skirt duty.

The whole world—everyone but me—seemed to be asleep as I dragged myself to the town green. I had never seen Frog Hollow so quiet, and it gave me the creeps. What if Mrs. Butterfield had meant nine o'clock instead of five o'clock? Then what would I do? When I reached the green, however, there was a flurry of activity. Still half-asleep, I stood in a daze at the edge of the green and watched the work crews setting up tents. When they finished, they stood in a circle drinking coffee from a thermos. Just then, I felt a fierce pinch on my arm.

"Ow!" I cried, pulling away.

It was Mrs. Butterfield—carrying a bullhorn. "AM I PAYING YOU TO STAND AROUND AND WATCH, BOY?" she said, her toothless mouth inches from mine. "GET TO WORK!"

I took a step backward. "I'm not getting paid," I protested in a small voice.

She rolled her eyes. "IT'S JUST A FIGURE OF SPEECH, BOY," she said irritably. "NOW GET TO WORK!"

She brought the bullhorn to her mouth and pointed it in my direction. "MOVE! MOVE! MOVE!" she yelled like a madwoman. I covered my ears and ran away from her deafening voice. Mrs. Butterfield was plumb crazy!

"NOW HEAR THIS!" she bellowed, pointing her bullhorn at the work crew on coffee break. "GET BACK TO WORK! SET UP THE STAGE! UNLOAD THE SOUND SYSTEM! PUT OUT THE TABLES! MOVE! MOVE! MOVE!"

The work crew looked up at Mrs. Butterfield with bewildered expressions on their faces.

"QUIT EYEING ME!" she screamed. "MOVE! MOVE! MOVE!" Then she saw me and yelled, "YOU THERE, BOY! MOVE! MOVE! MOVE!"

Jolted out of my sleepiness, I ran in one direction, but realizing it was the wrong way, turned and ran in the other direction. In my confusion, I crashed into someone carrying a stack of red tablecloths. We both fell in a heap to the ground, the tablecloths scattered about us in a jumble.

Groaning, I sat up and rubbed my neck. The other guy

sat up, too. He turned to me, and I gasped. It was Edgar the goon!

"Are you O.K.?" he asked earnestly.

"Uh, uh, uh," I stammered.

"You're not hurt, are you?" he said with concern.

"You're Edgar—Edgar the goon!" I exclaimed, then put my hand over my mouth in disbelief. The guy weighed about three hundred pounds and could kick my butt from here to Alaska and back. And I just called him a goon!

Edgar squinted at me. "You're Jackie, aren't you?" he asked mildly. He got to his feet and shuffled over to me. "I don't have my glasses with me," he explained.

"You better watch it," I said quickly. "I know karate." I had taken two weeks of karate when I was six years old, but I wasn't about to let him know that. I tried to get up, but my legs were paralyzed. Edgar was almost upon me. Instinctively, I covered my head and prepared to die. When nothing happened, I opened my eyes and looked up. Edgar was standing over me, holding out his hand. He had an amused expression on his face.

"I'm not going to hurt you," he said pleasantly. "Do you need help getting up?"

"Uh, no," I said, scrambling awkwardly to my feet. I quickly struck a karate pose, hoping I looked lethal. "Ki-yah!" I yelled menacingly.

Edgar ignored me and dusted off his pants.

"Ki-yah!" I yelled again.

Edgar turned to me. "What are you doing?" he asked.

"I'm warning you—I was the best in my class," I snarled. It was a lie. I was easily the worst.

Edgar bent down to collect his tablecloths. "You're not going to beat me up?" I asked in a disappointed tone.

He laughed. "Of course not. I have to do these tablecloths."

Slowly, I put my arms down. "Tablecloths?" I asked.

"I'm on tablecloth duty," he said.

"Tablecloth duty?" I repeated. "For Frog Hollow Day?"

Edgar nodded.

"But, but, you don't live in Frog Hollow."

"We're supposed to help out," he said.

"We?"

"The Brewster swim team."

My mouth dropped open. The Brewster swim team! That meant Cyrus the Virus might be lurking somewhere on the green!

"Why?" I asked in anguish.

"Coach—our coach—said we had to help because we used your pool." He gave me a smile. "Besides, it gives me a chance to see Mallory."

My cheeks suddenly burned with anger. "You better watch what you say about Mallory," I warned.

Edgar was still smiling. "She's wonderful," he said in a dreamy tone.

"Maybe you should just leave her alone," I growled.

Edgar looked at me. "You're on table-skirt duty, right?" he asked.

"Uh, yeah."

He made a motion with his hand. "Come on," he said. "We've got to do these before Mrs. Butterfield throws a fit."

The goon had a point.

I followed Edgar to the edge of the green. My eyes darted

crazily, trying to spot Cyrus the Virus. He could be anywhere—behind that oak tree, in back of the tents, under the boulders by the monument. In fact, this could all be a trick. Edgar could be lying about tablecloth duty. He could be leading me to Cyrus the Virus right now. With every step I took, I grew more panicked, until I was convinced Cyrus the Virus was going to rise out of the ground in front of me and punch me in the nose.

"You know, I was the *best* in my karate class," I said.

Edgar didn't respond.

"I won a trophy and everything."

Still no response.

"Maybe you should tell your friend Cyrus that," I hinted.

Edgar turned to me. "He's not my friend," he said with distaste.

"Yeah, well. Maybe you should tell him anyway," I said, wishing Cyrus the Virus would move to Siberia.

"Here are your skirts," Edgar said cheerfully, reaching into a cardboard box and handing me a bundle of white table skirts.

"Gee, thanks," I said.

"You're welcome," Edgar said with a smile.

I stared at him. It was a trick.

I followed the goon around the green, trying to stay as alert as possible. At each booth table, he laid down a red tablecloth, and I attached a white table skirt. We didn't talk as we worked, but my mind was filled with questions. When we finished, Edgar grabbed my hand and pumped it up and down like he was filling a bicycle tire.

"It was great working with you," he said breathlessly. "I

gotta go home now and help my little sister with her math project. She goes to a math camp for gifted children. I'll be back later. If you see Mallory, tell her I said hi. I can't wait to see her theme-park booth."

At the mention of Mallory, I snarled, "Stay away from her."

Edgar ignored me and stared into the distance. "I think I feel a poem coming," he confided to me in a whisper. Before I could stop him, he said in a high voice:

"The tablecloths are red,
The table skirts are white,
The sun shines on Frog Hollow,
What a beautiful sight."

He turned to me with a triumphant look on his face. "I went to poetry camp last summer," he said proudly.

I was too startled to speak.

"Good-bye, Jackie," he called as he walked away.

I lifted my hand to wave, but just held it there as though I were saying the Pledge of Allegiance.

I was still standing there with my hand raised when Nick, wheeling a cart loaded with flower baskets, came up to me. "Hey," he said glumly.

I turned to him in astonishment, putting my hand down at last. "You will not believe this, Nick! Edgar the goon just recited a really bad poem. And the Brewster swim team is here!"

Nick took out his comb and pulled it through his hair. "How long you been out here in the sun, Hemingway?" he asked.

"The goons are here!" I cried.

Nick finished with his hair and shoved the comb back in his pocket. "I got someone for ya," he said with a grin, changing the subject.

"What are you talking about?" I asked impatiently. The only thing I could think about was Cyrus the Virus, lurking around every corner—

"A girl, you dope," he said.

"A girl?"

"Yeah, you know." He made an outline of a girl's figure with his hands.

"Nick, forget it, there are goons here!"

Nick studied me. "Go home and chill out, Hemingway. Come back in a couple of hours and I'll introduce ya." He wheeled his cart away, grabbing baskets of flowers from it and placing one on each table.

"But the goons are here!" I yelled after him.

Nick waved me away with annoyance.

"The goons *are* here," I whispered to myself. I scanned the green once again for Cyrus the Virus. Maybe he had an early job like mine and had already gone home. Would he be back later?

By eight o'clock, the vendors had started to arrive, and the green got very crowded. I caught a glimpse of my parents hauling boxes to their booth. I also saw Mallory disappear behind the tents holding a banner that read "Theme Parks: Now and Then."

"Hallo, Jackie," someone said behind me.

I jumped and let out a shriek.

Garus, holding a garbage pick and dragging a trash can, looked startled. "What's the matter, old boy?" he asked.

"Nothing," I mumbled. "I thought you were . . . someone else."

Garus looked at the green. "Jolly good show, eh?" he asked.

"Yeah," I said absently.

"Do you know I got stuck this morning in the lift at my grandmother's flat? I almost did not make it here, old bean. I could use a nice cup of tea," he sighed, then added, "excepting that today is the day."

I nodded. I didn't have any idea what Garus was talking about.

"By the bye, what are you doing, old chap?" he asked.

"Looking for goons," I replied.

"Ah," Garus said. "A worthwhile activity, I should say. I better move on, then." He walked away, leaving me to study the green some more.

Chapter 20

> "Cal Lee Troy cursed himself for forgetting his horse—what use was a cowboy without a horse, especially when he had a bunch of stupid goons to outrun?"

I found myself composing opening lines in my head as I waited on the green for Charlene and Nick. I don't know how long I waited, but I soon saw Nick approach.

"Hemingway," he drawled, "I'd like to introduce you to someone very special." He stood in front of me with his luscious girlfriend on one side and another girl on the other.

"This is my friend, Jackie," he said to the girl in a formal tone. "He may not look like much, but he's a writer. That's why I call him Hemingway." He shot me a warning glance—the last thing he wanted was for me to start babbling about goons and poetry—especially in front of the ladies.

I scowled at his introduction. The girl turned a disinterested face to me.

"Jackie, this is Wanda," Nick went on. "Charlene's cousin."

She didn't look like Charlene. She didn't look like Kelly either. Nobody was as beautiful as Kelly. I frowned but changed my expression for politeness's sake.

Nick grinned with pride now that his work was done. "Shall we?" he asked Charlene, offering her his elbow. She took it with a giggle. I stared at them dumbly. When did Nick learn all these gentlemanly mannerisms? I wondered. In his spare time—when he wasn't combing his hair?

Nick steered Charlene toward the tents and left Wanda and me standing there. I briefly considered performing my own version of "Shall we?" but decided against it. Then, as if a signal had been given, Wanda and I both followed behind Nick and Charlene, walking side by side, a substantial distance apart.

"So, you're a writer?" Wanda asked.

I peeked at her again, trying hard not to compare her to Kelly but failing. "Yeah," I said noncommittally.

"Whatcha writing?" she asked.

I hesitated. "A novel," I finally said.

"What's it about?"

"I don't know," I said.

"You don't know?"

I turned to her. "No, I don't," I said.

"How could you not know?"

"What's it to you?" I asked irritably.

Wanda shrugged. "I don't know. I'm just trying to, like, make conversation."

I shrugged, too. I was losing interest in Wanda. Besides, I was still on the lookout for goons.

"I heard you went out with Kelly Phillips," Wanda suddenly said.

I stared at her. "Yeah," I replied casually.

Wanda smiled. "We used to be friends."

"Really?"

"Yeah, but not anymore."

"Why not?"

"I found out stuff about her that she doesn't want me to know," Wanda said.

I stopped midstep. "What stuff?" I asked.

Wanda shook her head. "I can't tell you," she said.

"Oh," I said, disappointed.

"But she would feel so bad if we ran into her, because she might *think* I'd told you."

I looked at Wanda and smiled. I scanned the crowd in front of us, hoping Kelly was out there somewhere.

Nick and Charlene had stopped in front of a cotton candy stand. Nick ordered a stick of fluffy blue cotton and handed it to Charlene with a flourish. Charlene squealed with delight.

"Do you want cotton candy?" I asked Wanda, hoping she'd say no. I only had a few dollars in my pocket and hadn't planned for this unexpected spending spree.

"No," she said. She pointed to the right. "I want caramel popcorn."

I frowned, then changed my expression quickly, but Wanda had seen my face. "You don't want to buy it for me?" she asked, sounding hurt.

"No, I do," I lied. "I really do."

We ambled over to the caramel popcorn stand, Nick and Charlene following us this time, and I bought Wanda the biggest tub they had, trying to make it up to her. She happily stuffed caramel popcorn into her mouth. "Want some?" she offered.

"O.K.," I said. She grabbed a fistful and thrust it into my mouth. We both laughed.

Next to the caramel popcorn was a stand selling foot-long hot dogs and lemon slushes. Nick treated each of us to a hot dog and a lemon slush, and the four of us stood in the center of the green gorging ourselves.

"Let's go on the Monster Whirler!" Wanda suddenly cried, her mouth full of popcorn and hot dog. She pointed at a dark-colored contraption that resembled a giant cockroach with its legs twisting this way and that. My face turned white. I hoped Charlene would say no, that it was a dumb idea, that it would mess up her hair, that Monster Whirlers gave her vertigo, that she had terrible cockroach phobia—anything.

"Yeah!" Charlene said.

I locked eyes with Nick. His face betrayed no emotion, yet he seemed to be saying, "I'm with you, pal, but we can't lose face in front of the ladies."

The hot dog and slush and popcorn felt like bricks in my stomach as I paid for two tickets. While we waited in line watching the Whirler make short work of others, my stomach began to tighten, as if getting ready to unload the lunch I'd just eaten.

Finally, it was our turn for the ride. Nick and Charlene sat side by side. Nick put his arm around Charlene's shoulders, and she leaned her head against him. Wanda and I also sat together, a full four inches between us.

I didn't have much time to think about whether or not I wanted to put my arm around Wanda, because the engines started to moan loudly and the Whirler began spinning. This isn't so bad, I thought, as we spun pleasantly on the ground, then lifted in the air and spun some more. I turned to Wanda. She was grinning widely.

Then the engines made an adjusting noise, and a louder, more urgent moan replaced the previous moans. Suddenly, without warning, the ride began spinning crazily, dipping and twisting and throwing us nearly upside down. I fought to hold on to the bar as my stomach sent up desperate warnings. Wanda screamed and grinned and looked at me with joy. I slid toward her without meaning to and stayed nearly on top of her for the rest of the ride. As much as I wanted to howl with terror, I kept my mouth closed and swallowed back nausea.

When the ride ended, my hair was sticking up in every way possible, my stomach was in rebellion, and I was practically in Wanda's lap.

"Wasn't that great?" Wanda exclaimed.

I nodded weakly and got up from the seat. Nick and Charlene followed, also enthusiastic. As we walked toward the exit, I bravely forced my feet to move, even though I felt I would collapse at any minute.

"Are you O.K., man?" Nick asked me.

"Fine," I croaked. I was holding my stomach and praying the nausea would pass. I breathed deeply, which helped a little.

Just then, Garus, holding his three golden retrievers on leashes, came walking toward us. Nick's eyes widened with horror. He tried to steer Charlene in the opposite direction, but it was too late. She had already seen them.

"Hi, Garus," she exclaimed. "What beautiful dogs!"

Garus stopped in front of her, and she knelt down and scratched each one behind the ears.

"What are their names?" she asked.

"That one's Gawain, this one is Lancelot, and this one's Galahad," Garus said proudly.

Charlene smiled. "You named them after the Knights of the Round Table?" she asked, and Nick's eyes widened even more. Garus had *re*named them after the Knights of the Round Table.

"I have always loved those enchanted stories," Garus said cheerfully, ignoring Nick's dirty looks.

Charlene smiled again. "I love your accent."

Garus beamed. "Thank you ever so much," he said.

"It was so *great* of you to bring your dogs *here*," Nick hissed, his voice dripping with sweetness.

"It was *nothing*, old boy," Garus replied in a similar tone.

Nick stared at him in disbelief. Then he turned to Charlene. "Uh, Charlene, babe, I, uh, want to show you something over there," he said, helping her up.

"Oh, but I just love these dogs," Charlene protested.

"Yeah, but this is such a cool thing," Nick said in desperation.

"What is it?"

"It's uh, uh, it's—" Nick turned to me for a suggestion.

"The Tunnel of Love," I offered helpfully.

Nick smiled with relief. "Yeah, the Tunnel of *Love*, baby." He put his arms around her.

Charlene looked in the direction Nick pointed. "Oh, can't we do it later, Nickie?" she asked. "I *love* these dogs." She knelt down again.

"I have three dogs, too," she told Garus, completely oblivious to Nick now.

"German shepherds," Garus replied.

"Yup. I *love* dogs."

"Me, too."

"I've always loved them."

"Me, too."

As I watched this scene, it suddenly occurred to me that Garus must have been planning this all along. That must have been what he meant by "today is the day." I couldn't blame him. He loved dogs. And so did Charlene.

Nick rose in a huff. His cheeks were bright red. He punched his fist into his hand twice. Garus, I figured, would get it later.

As much as I wanted to stay and see what happened next, I was starting to feel more and more nauseous. I had to sit down. It was then that my mother spotted me and shouted, "Hey, Jackie! Over here!"

I pretended I hadn't heard her and, still holding my stomach, turned to go in the other direction, where I'd spotted a bench. But Nick and Garus had looked up at the sound of Mom's voice and were now walking over to my parents' booth. Pretty soon everyone was heading to the holistic lifestyle booth, otherwise known as Weirdoland.

Chapter 21

> "Laid up in bed, he wondered how to live the next three months, since that was all the doctor had given him."

Mom waved furiously. "Hi, everybody!" she exclaimed.

I groaned and turned beet red. I would have rather eaten live scorpions than be seen publicly associating with Mom and Dad. I fervently wished the earth would just swallow me up and end this whole disastrous summer.

The booth looked more subdued than I thought it would. There was a big table with bottles and tubs and boxes everywhere, with pamphlets and signs that read, "Pantothenic Acid Can Relieve Hay Fever," and "Fish Oil Can Give You Smoother Skin," but there was nothing terribly outlandish about any of it.

"Who are these lovely young ladies?" Mom asked. She probably assumed they were girlfriends of Nick and Garus, since I had not informed my parents about my breakup with Kelly.

Nick's cheeks were still bright red, but he managed to get out a suitable introduction. "This is Wanda," he said, without enthusiasm. "And this"—he turned to Charlene with a look of betrayal on his face—"is Charlene." He glared at Garus. One of the dogs jumped up and tried to put his paws around Nick's waist. Nick jumped out of the way.

"Traitor," he mumbled through clenched teeth, directing his comment at Garus, who was ignoring him.

Still feeling nauseous, I murmured, "We should be going now."

"What's your hurry?" Mom said. "Have a protein shake first."

Oh, man. This had to be a nightmare. Soon I'd pop up out of bed in a cold sweat and see Mark, Isaac, and Dashiell swimming quietly in their tank. Mom shoved a paper cup into my hand. She poured brown liquid into four more cups and handed them to Nick, Garus, and the girls. Gawain, Lancelot, and Galahad barked noisily, as if wanting cups of their own.

"I feel nauseous," I said truthfully, declining my shake.

"Mmmm," Charlene said, taking a sip. "This is good."

"Yeah," Wanda added. "It tastes like chocolate ice cream."

I groaned and squeezed my stomach more tightly.

Nick and Garus finished theirs, and Mom poured them more. "This is great, Mrs. M," Nick said. "What's in it?"

I looked longingly at a Port-o-John in the distance. And then I saw them—Cyrus the Virus strolling toward the booth with Kelly Phillips on his arm! One look at Kelly's face and I could tell why she was stooping to associate with us. She wanted to rub Cyrus in my face. Coach and Mallory were right behind them. I groaned loudly, then dropped to the ground and hid under the table.

"Hi, Mallory!" Mom exclaimed. Mallory returned her greeting and introduced everyone. I crouched under the table, holding my stomach and wishing everyone would go away.

If Mom thought it was strange for Kelly to be with Cyrus, she didn't say anything about it. "Would you like to try a protein shake?" she inquired politely.

I didn't hear a response, but I heard Dad whirl the shake machine again. It suddenly occurred to me that no one had even realized I was gone.

"Mmmm," Mallory said.

Then I heard Kelly whisper loudly, "Don't drink that, Dad!" and I shot out from under the table. I don't know what made me do it, but I couldn't let Kelly Phillips—of all people—decide who should drink what at my parents' booth.

Kelly's eyes widened when she saw me. She snickered. I ignored her.

"Go ahead and drink it," I said to Coach. "It's not going to hurt you." Then I glared at Kelly.

Coach studied me silently, the cup poised in his hand. Then he tipped his head back and downed the drink in one gulp. He smacked his lips, banged the cup down on the table, and pronounced, "Delicious." He smiled at me, and I realized it was the first time he had ever done that.

Kelly's mouth dropped open. She stared at me, then at Wanda. Wanda smirked, and Kelly looked away, her cheeks bright red.

Cyrus the Virus stared at me, too. His eyes promised we would meet again under different circumstances. I ignored him.

"I'll buy a box," Coach announced.

Mom began filling his order. No one was paying any attention to me, but I was still as sick as could be.

It was Mallory who noticed my worsening condition. "Are you O.K.?" she asked kindly.

I moaned in response.

Mallory called my plight to Mom's attention, who regarded me briefly, bent down and reached under the table, and popped up with a handful of brown pills.

"Ginger capsules," she explained to everyone. "They relieve nausea, seasickness, any minor stomach ailments." A small crowd had gathered, and they nodded pleasantly, waiting for the lab hamster—me—to demonstrate. "Down the hatch, Jackie," Mom said to me.

"Why do these things always happen to me?" I whispered to no one in particular, aware that everyone had hushed and all eyes were on me.

"Down the hatch," Mom repeated, apparently unflustered by the attention.

I drank some water from a cup and swallowed the brown pills Mom handed to me. A silence so thick followed that I could have sliced it with a knife. Nobody spoke. Nobody moved. Suddenly, I felt better. I smiled.

Everyone smiled back and nodded enthusiastically, and a buzz of excited conversation ensued. Mom launched into a lecture on the benefits of natural remedies, mesmerizing the growing crowd.

"I'll take two cans of soy powder!" someone called out.

"Give me one, and some of that ginger, too!"

"How much for this nutrition book?"

I gazed dumbly at the scene before me, not able to make any sense of it. People were shelling out money for what my parents were hawking. I walked away from the booth, leaving Wanda to chat with Dad, leaving Nick and Garus to fight their battle for Charlene's affections, leaving Kelly to fawn over Cyrus. I needed to talk to someone. I saw Mallory returning to her booth, and I followed her.

Chapter 22

"'Take my advice,' she said. 'After all, it's free.'"

It seemed as though every child in Frog Hollow had received a secret invitation to come and see Mallory's booth. The place was swarming with children—grabbing everything with sticky hands, chattering a mile a minute, and designing their very own theme parks on construction paper.

Edgar was behind a table, cheerfully dispensing crayons and offering advice on the design of roller coasters and Ferris wheels. Mallory saw me and smiled. "M.p., you feeling better?" she asked.

"Yeah," I replied sheepishly.

I looked over my shoulder at my parents' booth, which was still busy with people. "I don't understand it," I said.

"What's there to understand?" Mallory said. "I told you they were ahead of their time. Their time has finally come."

I didn't know what she was talking about and was about to tell her that when she confided, "I mailed my essay out."

"The contest essay?"

"Yeah."

"That's great."

Mallory lowered her eyes. "Not really," she said. "It's not a winning essay. I tried my best, but I'm just not a writer."

I was about to say something comforting when her expression suddenly changed, as if a cartoon light bulb had turned on above her head. "Yes! Of course! Why didn't I think of it before?" she exclaimed, clapping her hands twice. She put her hands on my shoulders and faced me. Her eyes were filled with excitement.

"You're the writer!" she said. "*You* enter the contest, and we'll win for sure. We'll go to Kingdom of Magic!" She put a hand on her heart. "And I'll really be a theme-park designer someday," she whispered.

She gazed at me expectantly.

"Me?" I asked. "Enter your contest?"

"You just have to write an essay," she said, "on 'How I Spent My Summer Vacation.'"

"But I'm writing a *novel*." I said "novel" in a way that implied it was much more important than a contest essay.

Mallory seemed to notice this. "This novel, Jackie," she said in a voice dripping with sarcasm. "You're almost done with it, right? I mean, you've been working on it all summer."

I hesitated. "I can't get past the first sentence," I said, then looked down at the ground.

Mallory put a hand on my shoulder. "I know," she said. "Writing a novel is not easy."

"I'm going to do it," I said fiercely.

"I know you will," she said. "Someday. But not this summer."

I turned to her. "What do you mean?"

Mallory shrugged. "This summer you'll write an essay. You still have time before the deadline. And you have so much material!"

I didn't let her finish. "What are you talking about, Mallory? I'm not writing an essay. I'm writing a novel."

Mallory seemed confused. "I thought you said you couldn't get past the first sentence."

"Yeah," I admitted again.

"So, you're going to write an essay instead, right? You're going to start small and build up, right? Like your parents said?"

I was surprised. "My parents said that?"

Mallory looked at me like I was dumb. "Of course they did. Remember? At dinner? They said you have to start with projects that are the right size for you. Start with an essay or short story—*then* move up to a novel."

I didn't remember. I must have zoned them out—which I often did. It certainly sounded reasonable.

"So you're gonna do it, right?" she persisted. "You're gonna take their advice?"

"I don't need their advice!" I roared.

Mallory fell silent for several minutes. Finally, she spoke, and it was in a voice so sad I'd never heard it before. "You are so stubborn, Jackie," she said. "You won't take their advice because you say they're weird and don't know anything. Yet, look at that." She pointed to their booth. "Those people don't think they're weird. You're too stubborn to see that their advice is the right advice. I'm surprised you let Coach give you swimming advice—maybe you had no choice. But his advice worked, right?"

"That's different," I mumbled, but she ignored me and went on.

"You have to have an open mind to be a real writer."

I winced.

"You'll never be able to be creative if you're not willing to see things broadly. Or take advice from people who can help you." She studied me for several seconds, then turned back to her booth.

"Fine!" I said, not sure who I was talking to anymore. I stood there like an idiot for another minute, then walked home, my head pounding painfully.

When I got home, I went up to my room and sat down in front of the typewriter. I had an overwhelming desire to hack the machine to death with the ax my dad kept in the garage for chopping firewood. But instead I just sat there staring at the keys. I must have sat there for at least an hour.

And then it happened. I didn't mean for it to happen. But it did.

My brain opened up.

My parents, I thought suddenly, were not weird. They did *some* weird things, but they were not *all* weird. Kelly was beautiful, but she was as mean as . . . a snake. Edgar was big and awkward, but he was the nicest guy in the world.

My mind kept on dissecting the summer until I had a grasp on everything that had happened to me. Is this what not being rigid felt like? I fed in a piece of paper and typed: How I Spent My Summer Vacation.

I didn't get up from the typewriter until three hours later.

I had written nine pages. I reread them four times and liked what was there—no need to crumple up any more paper.

"Guys," I said to Mark, Isaac, and Dashiell. "I did it. I finally finished something."

Chapter 23

> "I thought the summer before high school would result in my writing the great American novel, but that's not what happened at all. What happened was better."

When my alarm clock went off at six o'clock the next morning, I felt the best I possibly could. I stretched happily, fed my fish, pulled on my bathing suit, and whistled all the way to the swim club.

I met Garus and Nick at the front entrance. An air of seriousness hung over the place like a fog.

"How you feeling, Hemingway?" Nick asked, fumbling with his comb. His hands were shaking.

"Great," I answered truthfully.

My enthusiastic answer caught him off guard. He put a clammy hand on my arm. "I'm glad you feel great, pal," he said soberly. Beside him, Garus nodded solemnly.

I nodded, too. I knew everyone was counting on me. After all, today was a big day for Frog Hollow—a huge day, a historic day. The Brewster swim team was here, and if we beat them, the long curse would finally be broken.

On one side of the pool I caught a glimpse of Cyrus the Virus and his goons. I saw Mallory on the other side. She waved and walked over. "Good luck, m.p.," she said. "I know you'll do great." She gave me a hug.

"Thanks," I said, then added, "I'm sorry about . . . you know." Mallory shrugged it off, and for the first time I realized what a truly great friend she was. In all the years I had known her, she had never once demanded an apology when I had acted like a jerk.

"Where's Edgar?" I asked.

Mallory blushed. "Well," she said. "He disqualified himself from the team."

"What?"

"He said he couldn't possibly try to beat Frog Hollow and be with me at the same time."

My mouth dropped open. I looked at Mallory's pink-cheeked face, and, for the first time all summer, I felt happy for her rather than jealous. And I realized that Mom and Dad *were* right—though we would always be friends, my relationship with Mallory *would* change in the next few years.

I remembered I still had to tell Mallory that I wrote and mailed my contest essay, but before I had a chance to, I saw Mom and Dad approach us.

"Jackie!" Mom exclaimed. She hugged me. "Good luck," she said into my ear.

Dad hugged me, too. "You're gonna do great!" he promised.

"I'm so glad you asked us to come," Mom said to me. "The phones are ringing off the hook, but I wouldn't miss this for anything."

"We couldn't let you win without a cheering section," Dad added.

Then Wanda suddenly appeared.

"I'm sorry I left you yesterday," I said to her.

"That's O.K.," she replied. "It gave me a chance to get to know your friend." She indicated Nick.

Just then, Coach's whistle brought us all to attention. We lined up at the pool as the crowd took their seats on the bleachers. Coach walked silently up and down the line. He stopped right in front of me.

"I have a good feeling about today," he said, looking right at me. "You boys are going to win." He smiled. I smiled back. Coach patted me on the shoulder. "Remember everything you've learned," he said to me. Then he announced, "Take five, then come back here and get into position."

We hung around the pool stretching and warming up. The sound of dogs barking startled me, and I turned around to see Charlene, who was holding six dogs on leashes and waving at Garus. Three of the dogs were Garus's, and three were hers. She blew Garus a kiss, and he blew one back. She moved to the side of the bleachers, the dogs in tow.

Nick gave Charlene a quick glance, then resumed his warmup. He and Garus had settled the "Charlene matter" yesterday. Nick had asked Charlene point-blank if she'd rather go out with Garus because of his dogs.

Charlene responded that people who truly loved dogs always got new ones when their old ones died, so where were Nick's new dogs?

Though Nick knew he was beaten, he couldn't resist one last attempt at gaining Charlene back, so he threw a punch at Garus. His punch was blocked by Galahad, who rose up on his hind legs with his slobbering mouth wide open. Nick's hand ended up inside Galahad's mouth. Garus made Nick promise to leave Charlene and him alone in exchange for letting Nick go home with his hand intact.

I guess Nick had that coming to him for a long time.

At the moment Nick and Garus were warming up right next to each other and seemed concerned only with beating Brewster. I was in the middle of my own warmup when I saw them—Cyrus the Virus and Kelly Phillips. She was giving him a long, slow kiss, and I felt physically ill. Then I heard her say, "Go and get 'em, Cy. Give 'em what they deserve." She gazed at me as she said this.

After kissing Cyrus, Kelly joined her girlfriends on the bleachers. Coach watched her go, looked at me curiously, then shook his head.

The short break was nearly up when the Brewster team moved into position next to us. As they approached, a sudden wave of panic flooded over me. Nick and Garus both stiffened, too. Cyrus the Virus cockily led the way, passing through rows of fearful Frog Hollow swimmers until he was towering right over me. I hadn't realized just how big he was. Power oozed from his very pores, making me feel very small and insignificant. Coach had told me earlier that I'd be racing him. It seemed O.K. then. Now I wasn't so sure.

Cyrus studied me with smoldering eyes for a full minute. I struggled to keep perfectly still, to keep my trembling hands at my sides, to keep my eyes locked with his. My knees were weakening, and I knew I wouldn't be able to hold the pose for long. But I lifted my chin a little higher.

A flicker of surprise crossed Cyrus's eyes. "See you in the water," he growled, then turned his back to me and walked to his lane, his entourage of goons proceeding to their own lanes.

Everyone breathed a collective sigh of relief. I silently watched Cyrus go, no longer concerned. My knees felt strong. My arms felt steady. I looked to my right, catching Coach's expression just before he could change it. It was one of pride, a "that's-my-boy" look.

Everyone moved into position. Garus would race first. I would be last. I waited patiently for my turn, concentrating on nothing but the water. We were doing well. Garus won his race, but Nick lost his. We were almost evenly matched with Brewster. By the time my turn came and I walked to the edge of the pool, we were tied.

I stood confidently beside Cyrus, no longer afraid of his bulk. The signal was given. We both dove into the water.

I swam exactly the way Coach had taught me. I didn't even think about it. I just swam automatically, cutting through the water like a shark. When I reached the other side I was surprised to see Cyrus still struggling toward the edge. I could take my time and still beat him. But I didn't take my time. I swam as fast as I could, using everything I'd learned from Coach.

When I finished the last lap, I knew I had set a record. The whistle blew. I climbed out. Boys gathered around me, slapping me on the back. Coach shook my hand, and everyone was cheering and screaming with joy. We had won! We beat Brewster!

Mom and Dad came bounding down from the bleachers. "We knew you could do it," Mom said.

Dad looked thoughtful. "Maybe it'll be swimming camp next year," he said.

I scowled. "I'm NOT going to any more camps," I said. "You may not believe this, but I *can* actually finish what I start. In fact, I wrote an essay. . . ."

Mom and Dad seemed confused. "Hold on, Jackie," Mom said in a quiet voice. "Did you actually think we were sending you to camp to deter you from writing?"

I paused. "Well, yeah," I finally said.

Mom and Dad glanced at each other in surprise. "We sent you so you'd get *ideas* for your writing," Dad said. "You don't get ideas cooped up in your room alone with a typewriter."

"You mean, you wanted me to write?" I asked incredulously.

"Sure," Mom said. "That's what you said you wanted to do. We wanted to help you."

My faced reddened. "I—I—I didn't know—" I began.

Mom smiled. "Well, now you know," she said, hugging me. I held onto her, suddenly grateful for everything that had happened this summer. It wasn't a waste of a summer at all. It was the best summer I'd ever had. Mom patted me on the back and then gazed at me. She smiled. "We're proud of you, Jackie," she said with tears in her eyes, and I was glad my face was already wet so she couldn't see mine.

"We'll see you at home," she said, and I made my way to the showers.

I was at the snack bar later when Kelly walked over. "You did great, Jackie," she said shyly.

"Thanks," I replied absently.

"Maybe we could, you know, get together later." She waited expectantly, her beautiful face radiant.

I studied her for a moment. "I don't think so," I said.

Her eyes narrowed. "It's not true," she said. "That's not it."

"What's not true?"

"What Wanda told you," she said.

"Wanda didn't tell me anything."

Kelly snorted. "It's not true. I really liked you."

I looked at her. She lowered her eyes. "It's just that your . . . family was so weird, I figured you would never . . ." She gazed at me. "Anyway, it's not true."

"I don't know what you're talking about," I said.

"I really did like you—I mean, I *do* like you. That thing with Cyrus was just . . . nothing. It's not the winning thing."

I was totally mystified. "Huh?" I said.

Kelly sighed. "Wanda knows I said I'd be going out with the winner at the end of the summer, but it's not true. I really liked you—"

I studied her, finally understanding. "You figured anyone who eats tofu and chants can't be a winner. But now that I beat Cyrus, you want to go out with me again?"

Kelly's face turned pale. "Didn't Wanda tell you?" she whispered.

"Wanda didn't tell me anything," I said. "You just gave it all away yourself."

Kelly put a hand over her mouth. I shook my head and walked away.

Chapter 24

> " This is the story of a boy, a girl, three goldfish,
> a swimming coach, and a python named Larry. "

I had four pages written before I had to leave for school. I sighed. "Never enough time," I said to Mark, Isaac, and Dashiell. I'd been writing so much, sometimes I'd forget I had other things to do—like go to school.

High school started months ago. Garus was with me in many classes, and so was Charlene. Nick wasn't; he fell in with a new crowd. Mallory went to a private school, and I didn't see much of her anymore.

Garus and Charlene were still hot and heavy. They even talked about getting married and someday opening up a dog-grooming business. Garus's English accent was stronger than ever, and a week before school, he announced he was to be called "Gary" and not "Garus" anymore.

It was nearly December when I met Nick coming home

from school one afternoon. He was walking Fifi. He saw me and smiled. "How you doing, Hemingway?" he asked. I liked it that he still called me that.

"Pretty good. How about you?"

"Not bad," he said.

"So, you like dogs," I observed.

"Yeah, it's funny," he said thoughtfully. "I did it for, you know, Charlene. But, now I just like them." He looked at me sheepishly. "You know," he went on, "sometimes you just have to try something. Have an open mind, you know?"

I nodded, surprised to hear such a profound statement from Nick. Just then, Tommy drove by in his wreck of a car and stopped at the curb in front of us. Two girls were in the backseat, and one was in front. They were all eating Pop Tarts.

"Nick, my man," he called out. "We're going snowboarding tomorrow, right?"

"You got it," Nick replied.

"How you doing there, Monterey?" Tommy nodded to me, then drove off.

Nick grinned at me. "My brother thinks I'm a lion tamer or something," he said, then lowered his voice. "He's still really scared of dogs."

I nodded again.

Nick looked at me. "We ought to get together," he said. "For, you know, old times' sake."

"Yeah," I agreed.

He smiled. "Maybe this winter break."

"O.K.," I said. "I'll see ya later."

I left him with Fifi and walked home. Mom and Dad

were meeting with the mayor about starting up a nutrition festival in Frog Hollow next year. The mail was in its usual place on the kitchen table, and I glanced through it absently. The return address on one envelope caught my eye. It said: "Kingdom of Magic. The Happiest Place on Earth."

"Could this be . . . ," I said to myself. I ripped open the envelope and read the letter quickly.

Dear Jackie,

We are pleased to announce that you are the grand-prize winner of our First Annual Young Writers Competition. Congratulations! You and up to five guests are invited to spend winter break at Kingdom of Magic. You'll be given a VIP tour. . . .

"Oh my God!" I yelled. I didn't read any further. Clutching the letter tightly, I raced out of the house. I stomped down the sidewalk, past Nick and Fifi. Looking over my shoulder, I called back, "We're going to Kingdom of Magic!"

"Who is?" he yelled.

"We are!" I responded.

By the time I reached Mallory's house I was panting crazily. I banged on her door like a madman, then stood back and tried to catch my breath.

She came to the door with a bewildered expression on her face. "Jackie?"

Edgar was standing behind her.

"Mallory, you're going! You're going to Kingdom of Magic!"

She looked confused. I shoved the letter in her hands, and she read it, her eyes widening with pleasure.

"You entered the contest?" she asked me.

"Yeah!" I laughed. "I never told you."

"Jackie!" She flew into my arms, dropping the letter on the ground. She kissed me, and a weird sensation went through me. Then she kissed me again.

"We're going to Kingdom of Magic!" she cried. She disentangled herself from me and picked up the letter. She waved it in front of her and began dancing on the sidewalk. When Nick and Fifi approached, she kissed Nick, too.

"We're going to Kingdom of Magic!" she yelled. "Do you hear me? We're going to Kingdom of Magic!"

Nick grinned. "It'll be like old times," he said, and I was thinking the same thing.